Enjoy!

The sequel to
THE FLOWER BOY

FLOWER POWER!

KEITH CAMPION

Illustrated by Catherine King

Matador
Unit E2 Airfield Business Park,
Harrison Road, Market Harborough,
Leicestershire. LE16 7UL
Tel: 0116 2792299
Email: books@troubador.co.uk
Web: www.troubador.co.uk/matador
Twitter: @matadorbooks

ISBN 978 1803136 691

British Library Cataloguing in Publication Data.
A catalogue record for this book is available from the British Library.

Printed and bound in the UK by TJ Books Limited, Padstow, Cornwall
Typeset in 11pt Minion Pro by Troubador Publishing Ltd, Leicester, UK

Matador is an imprint of Troubador Publishing Ltd

For my boys,
Leo & Artie
X

James wiped away tears of frustration with his sleeve. His school blazer was torn, the pocket hanging off and the white lining showing. Usually he would be acutely aware of everyone he passed in the street, but with adrenaline and anger cursing through him, the rest of the world might not have been there. His familiar walk – body stooped forward, head leading the way while his feet dragged along – took James rapidly through the streets of Hartlewich. Vague concerns filtered through his agitation – how much trouble would he be in? What would his mum and dad say? What would school say? But James didn't stop. He was stuck on a malfunctioning autopilot and he couldn't override it. His feet turned down a familiar street and a vision projected in his mind, like an old film reel flickering into life.

It was a school field, basking in the summer sunshine. Everything was bright and dazzling, heat shimmered on the yellowing grass. There was the unmistakable sound of children laughing and shrieking in a rhythm of happy play. Above, a weather front was delivering an almost perfect line of grey cloud. It slowly covered the sun, causing a shadow to sweep across the field, dampening the excitable atmosphere like a blanket. Spots of rain began to fall. Huge drops – a warning of the inevitable downpour about to happen. There were screams and the midday assistants sprang into action, calling and wafting their arms to usher everyone towards the school building. Children began to dash across the field from all directions as the rain started to pound down. One little boy, in shorts and t-shirt, was still standing in the middle of the field unmoving – his blank expression masking the panic inside him. Plastering his hair to his head, the rain streamed down his face. Another midday assistant rang a bell furiously at the remaining stragglers, and the last few children thundered past him. The boy stepped back a few paces. The doors of the school building were pulled closed with a thump and the boy turned and ran in the opposite direction, to the trees and bushes at the top of the field. Pushing aside the branches of a thick bush, he clambered inside and sat down on some dry leaves with his back to the wire fence. Calm descended over him, as he peered across the field from his shelter.

James's pocket vibrated and the film ended abruptly. He reached for his phone, hesitated, then slipped it back in his pocket and carried on down the pavement, avoiding the cracks like he'd always done.

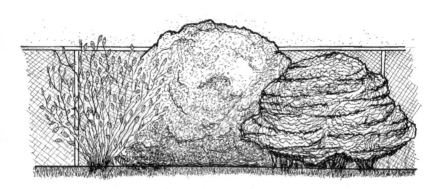

Chapter 1

A ball of tightly wrapped paper smacked James on the back of the head. It stung and made him jump. Whoever had screwed it up had done a thorough job to create the hardest strike possible. There were sniggers from behind him. Malika attempted a supportive smile from across the table, but James noticed her glance over to where a group of girls were sitting. He could read her thoughts. James fiddled with the pencil case in front of him. The art teacher, Mrs Sims, was at the front of the classroom with her back to the class. Rummaging through a pile of work, she tutted to herself.

James had been at high school for over six weeks. Leaving behind the security of his village primary school, he was desperately missing everything he once knew. James lived a narrow life – the two places he had felt safest were home and school. Anything else outside of these two places was a step out of his comfort zone. Fifty per cent of his safe spaces had gone when he left primary school. He knew it was going to be tough for someone like him, but nothing could have prepared him for the monumental impact moving to high school was going to have on him. Other children seemed to be taking it all in their stride, making new friends and adapting with ease. There was no *outward* sign that James was in turmoil, he was his usual introverted self – but the sheer effort of getting through the day while trying to appear as normal as possible was exhausting him. James lived his life in a state of high anxiety and it tired him out just being *him*. That morning, it had been the Year 7 assembly and they had sung the song 'Autumn Days'. James had to do everything in his power not to start sobbing. It was a song they had sung many times at primary school and the reminder was almost too much to bear. Primary school wasn't perfect for James, but it was what he had known for seven years. A secure and consistent place with routines, structure and boundaries he had learned to understand and cope within.

Having a complete inability to talk to people was always going to be an issue when he was meeting new pupils from other primary schools. Amongst twelve hundred high school pupils, he was invisible. At least at primary school, Mrs Shah had made him feel like *somebody*, like he was valued and had something to offer despite his near silence. Now, each morning, his stomach churned until he felt sick and he convinced himself he wasn't going to be well at school. His mum, Sally, had to reassure him about where she would be that day, just in case she was required to come and collect him. He also needed to visit the toilet much more – to find some space away from the classroom on his own. Noticing the frequency of these visits, some teachers wouldn't give him permission to go, clearly believing he was trying to waste lesson time.

Mrs Sims was still sifting through the pile of artwork. The class had been asked to draw a piece of fruit with a soft pencil to show their shading skills.

"Ok, settle down, settle down. As I was saying, it's really not good enough 7G. You must put more effort into your homework. This is a wake-up call. You are not primary school children anymore – you are at high school now and we expect more from you."

The table of boisterous girls were gesturing at Malika and pointing at a spare stool at the bench they were sitting around. Malika was the girl everyone wanted to be friends with. She was tall, her hair was always in a topknot and she was bubbly and effortlessly cool. For a reason he never understood, Malika had taken James under her wing in the last year of primary school. In the summer holidays they had met up a few times and it'd been ok. James had even managed to talk. But the shock of the new school had sent the speaking part of his brain back into a deep freeze and his confidence around Malika had evaporated.

"Sorry James, I'm just going to, erm…I'm sorry." Pointing sheepishly at the other table, Malika picked up her pencil case and reached for her bag off the floor. She skulked over – sitting down on the stool to a couple of welcoming whoops from the other girls. James gulped. It hurt – but he kept his face expressionless. He didn't blame Malika for moving, he could see he was holding her back.

The same thing had happened with Tom. James had started the year walking to school each morning with Tom. They had a chequered history. James considered them complete opposites – he was tall and thin, with a long fringe hanging over his eyes, Tom was shorter and stockier with closely cropped hair. James was painfully shy and avoided social contact, whereas Tom was brimming with self-belief. James was pretty much ignored by everyone, but Tom was popular and picked for all the sports teams. Tom had not been particularly nice about James's passion for growing roses earlier in the year. Eventually he helped James in his mission to remember the people of the village in the churchyard by placing the flowers James had grown at their forgotten graves. Tom still called James 'The Flower Boy' now and then, but James didn't mind because Tom said it in a different tone than he used to. James and Tom had both been placed in Mr Fellows' tutor group. James wondered whether it was Mrs Shah's suggestion. Had she spotted their growing friendship and hoped it was a developing bond?

Tom had clearly started to find it hard work being around James. Seeing a distance was forming between them again, James was completely unable to do anything about it. After a few weeks, Tom texted to say he was going to start getting a lift into school so that he could get up a bit later. James liked to go into school earlier, to miss the crowded pavements and the rush of traffic. One morning he had been a little bit later than usual because his baby sister, Jessie, had slept in and no one had the heart to wake her. James hated any change to his routine and left for school in a flap. Walking ahead of him was Tom with some new friends he had made.

James's start at high school had an inevitability even he could have predicted. It went wrong from the very first morning. Their tutor, Mr Fellows, was doing a 'get to know the class' activity. James hated this type of thing with a passion. To make matters worse, Mr Fellows was picking who went next by pulling names on lolly sticks from a jar. James was uncomfortable being put on the spot. He couldn't talk in front of people, especially with little warning. When Mr Fellows asked him what his 'likes' were, James felt thirty pairs of eyes burrowing into him. He couldn't say he liked spending time at churchyards, he didn't think that would go down well at all, so he blurted out he played with Lego sometimes. Cue the snorts of derision from his new classmates. He didn't even know why he said it. He barely ever played with Lego – he'd panicked. He also failed to add it was the technical Lego kits that even his dad found challenging to build, but he'd said it and had to face the consequences.

"Is Jamesey-Wamesey going to play with his Lego-Wego tonight?" asked a boy called Josh, in his best baby voice when they went to lunch. Josh was one of the boys Tom had become pally with. He was taller than Tom, had the latest fashionable haircut and walked around school with a swagger.

Mrs Sims turned again, satisfied she'd found the piece of work she had been looking for.

"Just look at this one. There's no effort here. I think it's supposed to be a banana – it's not one that I would eat any time soon." The class guffawed. "Come on 7G – you need to raise your game!"

It was James's work. He wanted to sink right down into his chair and disappear. He *had* tried. He'd *really* tried. Agonising over which fruit to pick, he'd gone through seven different pieces of paper to get a drawing he was even remotely happy with. By the end he'd been in tears at the kitchen table. Sally had told him to stop. It wasn't worth it, she'd said. He'd just have to explain he'd found it difficult and that art wasn't his thing, but he'd appreciate help and would work hard to improve. There was no chance James was going to approach a teacher he barely knew and say all that. He sighed and put his head on his hands.

"Sit up James, please!" Mrs Sims barked.

Chapter 2

Over the last year, James had developed a strong friendship with Mrs Samuel, an old lady who lived in the village. They had met at the village churchyard while she was putting flowers on her husband's grave and James had become engrossed in her stories about the village's history. James used to visit the churchyard regularly on his weekend walks around the village. It was one of the few places where he felt at ease. Mrs Samuel struggled with her memory regarding day-to-day tasks, but James would ask her about something that happened fifty years ago and she'd have a crystal clear recollection.

James had become worried that Mrs Samuel was finding life a challenge and he felt she needed help. He had written to her only child, John, in the hope that he would offer a bit more support. James had only met John a couple of times since then and found him aloof on each occasion. John made James feel like he had done something wrong, even though he didn't have a clue what it was. John was tall and burly, reminiscent of the pictures

James had seen of his dad, Harry. But while Harry always had a toothy grin on his face, John had a perpetual frown on his. He had thick black eyebrows and dark stubble. James thought he must be around fifty years old, and he always wore trousers and a shirt which made him appear like he had just come from a business meeting.

When Mrs Samuel couldn't get to the churchyard anymore, James had started visiting her at her semi-detached home on a Saturday afternoon instead. 2pm on the dot – the same time Mrs Samuel always went to see Harry's grave. James would take her a few bits and bobs for her kitchen cupboards and make her a cup of tea. Sometimes Mrs Samuel would chat away happily, other times they would watch TV in quiet companionship. When Mrs Samuel spoke, she often repeated things she had already mentioned. She was none the wiser and James would patiently react in the same way each time. A couple of times she had asked James how school was going and he'd tried to be positive, but she saw through it.

"You just be you, son," she said. "Be true to yourself and don't put on any airs or graces for anyone. If they don't like it, they can take it or leave it."

They all *did* leave it, James thought. No one wanted to know him.

"Put a record on when you go, son. One from The Beatles, that'll do," Mrs Samuel would always say when it was time for James to go. Mrs Samuel had a huge record collection and she'd inspired James to create 1960s playlists on his phone to listen to while he walked.

Mrs Samuel couldn't work the record player anymore, but James had become an expert and loved the whole process – it was far more satisfying than searching for a song on an app. He adored the old albums with their interesting covers and the track-listing on the A side and the B side of the record. He'd slide the vinyl out and hold it, full of promise for the music it held in its grooves. Making sure the A side was facing up, he placed it on the record player. He'd lower the needle and wait for the warm crackle through the speakers before the first song played.

James hadn't visited Mrs Samuel for a few weeks. Worries about school and not wanting to bump into John Samuel kept him away, and he'd started making excuses to his parents as to why he wasn't leaving the house. The last couple of Saturdays when James had arrived at Mrs Samuel's house, John's car had been parked outside. James carried on walking and didn't call in. He couldn't face it. Even John's car was scary. It was large and black, had a personalised number plate and looked very shiny and new. Since starting at high school, James had lost his motivation to go for his usual walks too. Everything seemed like so much effort, even the churchyard didn't have the same appeal. He wanted to be at home when he wasn't at school, but he felt guilty about not seeing Mrs Samuel and he missed her too. He knew he needed to visit her, and if John was there he'd just have to say hello and leave as soon as possible. At least he would have been – he didn't want Mrs Samuel to think he had stopped caring, or forget who he was.

Luckily, the perfect incentive to get himself out of the house and go round presented itself. James had established the Hartlewich History website when Mrs Samuel told him no one was interested in running the local historical society any more. Not wanting village history to be forgotten, he started recording the information Mrs Samuel had described to him and blogged about it online. Recently, someone had posted a picture of men from the local works on the website. Camaraderie spilled out of the black and white photo – the men grinned and put their thumbs up for the camera outside one of the factory buildings. James spotted Harry Samuel instantly amongst them – he thought Mrs Samuel would love to see the photograph.

Deciding to call in after school one day, James figured John Samuel would be at work during the week so there would be less chance of bumping into him. As James approached Mrs Samuel's semi-detached house, he could sense its emptiness almost immediately. A 'For Sale' sign was hammered into a flower bed in the front garden and the grass was long. All the curtains had been removed from the windows making the house look cold and deserted.

Walking up the drive, James could see the lounge was empty. He opened the letterbox with a squeak and peered in. The black and white photograph of Harry and Mrs Samuel when they were courting had been removed from the hall wall, and there was a rectangle of cleaner wallpaper where it had been. Where was Mrs Samuel? James hoped she was ok – he knew she was getting older and frailer. He hadn't seen her move from the old armchair in her lounge during any of his most recent visits, but surely he'd know if anything had happened to her?

"Mum, Mrs Samuel… Mrs Samuel has gone," James blurted out, arriving back at his house. Standing at the kitchen counter, a brown envelope ripped open next to her, Sally was deep in thought as she read a printed letter.

"Hmm has she, love?" Sally replied. Her focus switched from the letter to James and she looked confused. "Gone? Gone where?"

"I don't know," said James, more urgently, not really feeling like the matter was getting the attention it deserved. "Her house is empty, there's… there's nothing there. All her things have gone – her whole life. Her life with Harry has gone. The house is for sale. Where is she?"

"That's really strange, love," Sally replied, folding the letter and placing it in a drawer. James caught sight of some bold, red writing.

"How can she just disappear without us knowing? What can I do?"

James was furious with himself for not going round sooner.

"It's ok love, try not to worry. We'll look into it. I'm sure if she could, she would've said what was happening. Didn't you say she had a son?"

"John. John Samuel," James said solemnly.

"Well, I can take a peek to see if he's on Facebook, send him a message and try to get to the bottom of it."

James felt slightly reassured by this.

"Why didn't *he* try and contact us? He knew I went round to see her," asked James.

Before his mum could answer, James's baby sister toddled unsteadily into the room followed by their dad, Paul.

"Jay, Jay!" she called.

Jessie was grinning at James and looking very proud of herself. She crashed into his legs and clung onto his jeans unsteadily. James reached down and heaved Jessie up and held her. She put her hands on either side of his face and he blew out his cheeks for Jessie to push together, causing a raspberry sound. Although she had done this many times, she still found it hilarious.

Paul glanced at the brown envelope in Sally's hand as she put it in the bin.

"Jessie's becoming a bit of a nightmare now she can walk. I can't keep up with her. I'm sure you weren't this much trouble, James," Paul said. "Want to come out into the garden with us?"

James followed them through the back door. He watched Jessie lumbering after a cat which had entered the garden, and was now the target of her unwelcome attention. James thought about Mrs Samuel and how she had inspired him to learn how to grow roses earlier in the year. He'd become totally obsessed by this task – it had meant so much to him. It was only six months ago, maybe a little longer, but it seemed like a different lifetime. So much had happened since then and he hadn't thought about his roses for a while now. Even though winter was on its way, he probably should have been doing something with his flower beds, maintaining them and getting them primed for more blooms next year. He didn't have the heart. He didn't have the heart for anything, and now he'd lost Mrs Samuel too.

Chapter 3

Although he was one of the tallest in Year 7, James walked between lessons with his head down, his mop of hair hanging over his eyes, hoping that no one would pay him any attention. They didn't, mostly. The lessons were ok; he loved learning and he liked the new organisational elements of high school like keeping folders of work and his homework diary. Some of the teachers made efforts to engage him in conversation but whenever James was spoken to his heart skipped a beat, he panicked and the teachers could clearly see he was uncomfortable so they moved on. He'd then spend the rest of the day beating himself up inside for this exchange, or lack of it.

James started to view the day in bite-sized chunks to help him cope, setting himself the goal of getting to first break without even contemplating the rest of the day. His next milestone would be to get to lunch, then the end of the day. A second clock in his mind was monitoring how far it was to the end of the week – he'd break it into days, lessons, lunchtimes. The thought of the security of a Friday evening at home was his ultimate target and for those few hours at the end of the week, he felt relaxed. He could enjoy Saturdays, but Sunday was on his mind. Sunday meant school the next day – so Sundays were spent worrying about the week ahead. It was just Friday evening really; a few hours of the week where James felt genuinely anxiety free. With all this ticking over in his mind, James felt drained at the end of each day. He wanted to sit and flick through the news on his phone, or watch something on TV. He found the increased levels of homework a challenge and didn't seem to have the focus each evening – something his parents had commented on a few times. There was another thing James was finding tricky – he'd developed a few spots. Not a big outbreak like some of his friends, but a few on his nose. Whereas most people could accept that this was part of growing up, a spot could push James over the edge and mean he couldn't even face leaving the house until it was gone. He found looking in a mirror difficult at the best of times and hated catching himself in a reflection, but now he'd spend hours at the mirror staring at the smallest pimple, willing it away. Convincing himself it was all anybody would see if they looked at him, it made him shrink into himself even more.

There were some things he liked: English lessons and maths. There were some things he definitely didn't like: any time where there was a lack of structure – moving between buildings, lining up to enter a room, getting changed in PE – these were all stressful. James hated partner work too. He dreaded the class being asked to find someone to work with and being the one left over. He'd either be asked to join another pair to make a three, or someone would roll their eyes when they realised James was the last option. He always worked happiest on his own.

James didn't dislike exercise. He could walk for hours at pace and barely break into a sweat. Walking had become a kind of therapy to him during his final year at primary school. But James hated *sport* at high school. Whereas PE lessons at primary school had been fun and something to look forward to, PE at high school seemed much more serious with an unpleasant undercurrent of competitiveness. Just the thought of the changing rooms made him shudder – the odour of mud and the dread of the unsupervised rowdiness. James had taken an instant dislike to the PE teacher, Mr Ramos, who always seemed so pleased with himself. PE lessons were a boys' club James and the less sporty children were only tagging along to. They were present, but not members. Mr Ramos enjoyed the sound of his own voice far too much for James's liking. He had his hair perfectly waxed and had grown designer stubble. He'd often talk about his own sporting achievements, whilst scanning the boys in front of him to check they were suitably impressed by his triumphs. The football team he played for, rugby, you name the sport, Mr Ramos was a top player – according to him. It came as a surprise to James that he had any time left to teach PE at all in his busy life of sporting prowess.

Mr Ramos would gather in a huddle with the more talented boys who would laugh loudly at him and it all seemed very cliquey. James knew he would never, ever be part of that huddle. Observing this also made James realise something about himself he had never really considered before. He had no laugh. That's not to say he didn't find things funny, but while other children had their own spontaneous 'laugh out loud' laugh, no sound came out of James's mouth. He was *even* invisible when he found something funny.

On one particularly cold Autumn afternoon, the class were having a football lesson on the field. The school had pitches for a number of sports behind the building. They sloped downwards, and beyond the trees was the most incredible view across the county plain to the hills in the distance. The class were practising chipping the ball and trying to get it as high as they could. James had never been into football. He'd sometimes watch a match if his dad had a big game on the TV and he enjoyed the atmosphere, but he'd never got involved in playing. The idea was to loft the ball over someone in the middle to the person on the other side of a grid marked with cones. No matter how hard he tried, James couldn't get the ball more than a foot off the ground. Aware that others had stopped their own game to watch his flailing efforts, he could feel the dread rise throughout his body. His legs started to wobble which made the chipping attempts even more laughable. He heard the sniggers. When Mr Ramos called them back to him James overheard Josh, one of Mr Ramos's clique, turn to Tom and sneer that James looked like a giraffe on stilts. Tom was always the one called out to demonstrate with Mr Ramos. He could make the ball glide gracefully to wherever Mr Ramos asked him to direct it.

When James got home that afternoon he flung his bag to the floor and plonked himself down at the kitchen table, slumped and sighing. Paul appeared out of the study at the end of the hallway. They called it 'the cupboard' because although it had a small desk and a swivel chair, it was too small for anything else. If Paul stretched backwards his arms caught the wall behind him. Paul wandered across the kitchen and flicked the switch on the kettle. He looked down at his phone, pulled a face and slid it into his pocket.

"Everything OK, Champ? Good day?" he leant on the kitchen surface and folded his arms.

James made a face which he hoped said 'as if!' and without looking up, he pulled out his own phone and started flicking through the notifications on his apps.

"You could actually speak to me with more than a grunt now and then, James. I get you might not have had the greatest of days, but you might not be the only one." Paul grabbed a cup out of the cupboard causing a few of them to clink together and banged it down of the surface. He picked up a teabag out of the jar and threw it in the cup. He didn't wait for the kettle to finish boiling, sploshing the water into the cup and spilling some on the kitchen surface. James tried to pull a suitable face of concentration to deter any more questions.

"So what's up?" Paul tried again, trying to soften his tone but realising he still sounded confrontational. He was in too deep to stop.

"It's just boring. I… I don't like school." James felt exposed when anyone looked at him for too long.

"For goodness, sake, James. How can it be boring?

You study all those different subjects, all those topics. How can *that* be boring?"

James felt frustration rising within him but he didn't have the fight.

"I'm going to my room," he muttered, getting up and walking out of the door with pretend nonchalance.

"So you're not going to talk? James is just going to do what he always does – hide in his room. Off you go then. Great that is, James," Paul called after him. He waited a moment, then leaned against the kitchen surface and screwed his eyes tightly shut.

Closing his bedroom door behind him, James sat on the edge of his bed. He shook his fringe down over his face, something he did when he was upset – it was an extra layer to hide behind, another barrier to the world. How could he explain that life was such an effort for him, and when he got home he *hated* questions? He needed an hour, an hour of head space to file the day's events away and wind down. He didn't blame his dad for his reaction. James knew he had been rude, but sometimes he wanted to be on his own. It wasn't a personal insult to anyone, it was just what he needed to cope.

Chapter 4

Lessons always followed a similar pattern for James. He'd make his way through the school corridors, holding his breath and praying he wouldn't become the target of any kind of attention. Once in class, it would take him the first fifteen minutes to settle into it. If he was lucky, he'd then get thirty minutes where he'd focus and absorb the lesson – as long as he wasn't asked to speak or put on the spot, he'd be fine. Then the last fifteen minutes of the lesson would be a build-up of anxiety knowing he had to navigate the corridors again to get to his next class.

That was how it was when his English lesson ended one wet Monday morning. Waiting until everyone had shuffled their way out of the classroom, James purposefully placed his books into his bag as slowly as possible to avoid the scrum. His English teacher looked up and smiled at him as she rearranged some piles of paperwork, but she didn't say anything. When he exited the doorway onto the busy corridor, the hive of activity compared to the calm classroom was a shock to the system. It suddenly dawned on him that he had no idea where he was supposed to be next. Children bustled around him and James started feeling his pockets for his timetable, trying to remain calm. Was it science or maths? He'd been there a few weeks and thought he knew his timetable off by heart, but he had a mental block. Hating any uncertainty, he cursed himself for not checking his timetable was in his blazer pocket as usual. He remembered in Year 6, when Mrs Moores from the high school had visited them, someone asked what would happen if they didn't know where they were supposed to be. It was funny then, it wasn't funny now.

The timetable definitely wasn't to be found and his throat tightened. He was already going to be late and have to walk into the room last with the class watching him, and maybe have to explain to the teacher in front of everyone what had happened. He also wouldn't be able to cope with the humiliation of arriving at the wrong lesson if he took a guess at where he was supposed to be. The corridor was now getting quieter and tears pricked his eyes. As he bent down and scrabbled through his bag again, there was a familiar voice above him.

"All ok? Jamie, is it? Late for your next lesson?"

James looked up to see Mr Ramos standing before him. He was holding a mug that said, 'This is what an awesome PE teacher looks like'. James wasn't surprised that Mr Ramos got his name wrong. This kind of thing happened to him a lot. If someone called him by the wrong name, he rarely had the confidence to correct them. James always wanted to be forgettable so he couldn't complain.

"My timetable, I can't find it. It's not in my pocket, or

bag. I… I really need to find it." James was furious with himself when a tear escaped his eye.

"Come on Jamie, follow me. You're not the first and you won't be the last. We'll get ourselves to the office and they'll do some quick computer trickery, print you off a new timetable and you'll be on your way to your next lesson in no time."

James followed in Mr Ramos's wake as he strode down the corridor, booming a hello at some pupils, telling others not to run, picking others up on their uniform – a shirt hanging out, or a loose tie. Once they'd visited the office, he handed James his newly printed timetable.

"Right, you're good to go. Best get to that science lesson."

"Thank you," James said, but didn't move.

Mr Ramos looked at him and narrowed his eyes.

"You're worried about walking in late aren't you?"

James nodded.

"Totally understand, I wouldn't want to either. It's like when you walk into a restaurant and everyone turns and looks, I hate that. Look, I can't take you there because I've got a class myself. Take a deep breath and walk in that room with your head held high. Just say to yourself, 'I'm big, I'm strong, I'm brave'. Say it to me now, out loud."

James pulled an awkward face and Mr Ramos laughed.

"No, I wouldn't do *that* either. So just think it in your mind when you walk in that room. Knock on the door, take a big breath and think 'I'm big, I'm strong, I'm brave'. Apologise for being late and sit yourself down like it's not a problem."

Mr Ramos ambled off down the corridor, whistling and tossing an apple up and down. Finding his way to his science class, James took the suggested deep breath and knocked on the door. He mumbled a quick apology and felt the class's eyes on him. He repeated Mr Ramos's advice in his head over and over again.

Chapter 5

James was perched on a bench next to the school building. He opened his Tupperware box, placed it on his knees, and took out his sandwiches. Unwrapping them and nibbling at them, he kept his head down, glancing up from time to time at the game of football that was taking place on the square of tarmac in front of him. It was cold, and brown leaves swirled around his feet. The boys were booting a tennis ball around. Tom's talent stood out a mile as he ran rings around the others. Tom was currently enjoying school celebrity status because he had been scouted and was now training with one of the big local football club's youth teams. James was pleased for him.

Clearly frustrated at being nutmegged again, Josh kicked out, catching Tom on the shin as he swept the ball past him. Tom stumbled but continued, taking it past another boy and sliding it past the goalkeeper just inside the school bag which had been placed down as a post. He turned away laughing and kissed the school badge on his blazer in celebration. It wasn't like James to get close to others at lunch but he felt slightly safer around Tom, even if Tom had reverted back to ignoring him. Sally and Paul had urged James to try and make a bit of effort with others, so at least he could say he spent lunchtime with the footballers even if it wasn't 100 per cent accurate. There was no chance he was going to go into the dinner hall for lunch; he couldn't stand the noise and the unpredictability of hundreds of teenagers crammed into a room.

Putting the sandwich crusts back in his box, James lifted out a large yellow pear his mum had packed for him and stared at it in disbelief. Fair enough trying to encourage him with his five-a-day, but as if he was ever going to eat a huge mushy pear in front of people at school. He was the world's most self-conscious eater at the best of times, never mind with pear juice dribbling everywhere. He placed the offending piece of fruit on the bench ready to throw in the bin with the rest of his rubbish when he'd finished. He opened a chocolate biscuit instead – it was one of the ones designed to look almost exactly like the top brand, but half the price. James wondered what Mrs Samuel would be doing at that moment. It was strange not even knowing where she was, and he hoped Sally had got somewhere with her messages to John Samuel.

As James contemplated this, he suddenly tuned back into what was going on around him and noticed the game in front of him had paused. A few of the players were in a huddle in the middle of the tarmac area. There seemed to be a whispery discussion which concluded with a high-pitched laugh. Josh said something to Tom, who peered behind him at James with an uncertain look on his face. James felt uneasy and shifted in his seat, sensing danger. He put his half eaten biscuit back in the box and clamped the lid on and slid the box into his school bag on the floor between his legs. James was good at picking up on an atmosphere and was an expert at reading body language – this came from years of watching conversations around him rather than being part of them. Tom turned and started walking over and the boys watched, trying to supress their grins. Tom sat down next to James.

"Hey, James. You ok? How's things? Doing ok? What… erm… what you up to?"

James went to answer but the words got caught in his throat and the warning alarm in his head got louder and louder. The other boys wandered over, trying too hard to look like everything was normal.

"We should meet up sometime… erm… go for a walk or something. Maybe meet at the church?" Tom continued.

James nodded, barely taking in what Tom was saying as the other boys arrived. One of them put their arm around Tom playfully, another stood in front of James, and Josh was out of James's vision at the other end of the bench. James was trapped. Through the tangle of bodies, he was just able to see Josh come back around in front of him and pull his arm back.

"Now! Out the way!" Josh shouted.

Tom shuffled up the bench and the two other boys sprang to the side. James had time to see that Josh had something in his hand and it was being launched at his head at full pelt. He thought it was the tennis ball they'd been playing football with, but it only took a millisecond to realise what was about to hit him was his mum's over ripe pear. James had little time to react, managing to turn slightly and attempt to get his hands up for protection. The pear exploded against the side of his head. It disintegrated over him and the wall behind. James shot up, gasping, covered in pear gunk. Instinctively wiping his face and hair, he shook his hands down, flicking sticky gloop to the ground. He was covered. The boys around him were momentarily silent, a look of shock – mixed with glee – on their faces. After a few seconds, they broke into hyena laughs. James tried to laugh because he didn't know what else to do. Tom was laughing too, but also brushing some sticky juice from his own blazer.

Other pupils started to gather around and James had no idea what he was going to do next – everyone was looking at him. Reaching down he instinctively grabbed his bag and marched forward across the tarmac to more laughter around him. Behind him, he heard the familiar and distinctive voice of Malika.

"What's happened? Where is James going? What have you done to him?"

He heard Tom replying and Josh saying something in a defensive tone.

"That is not OK. How dare you do that?" Malika shouted.

The atmosphere behind James changed from a raucous buzz to confusion as he got further away from them. He couldn't stop himself. Striding up to the fence at the side of the concrete area, he threw his bag over then hauled himself up. He felt something rip as he pulled himself over the top. He landed heavily on the other side. Without turning, he picked up his bag and made his way down a side street towards the main road. James could hear Malika's distant voice at the fence, pleading with him to come back.

Chapter 6

Sally placed her phone down on the kitchen surface and put her hand to her brow, scrunching her eyes together tight.

"Paul, James has run off." She didn't shout it. She said it slowly, in a 'let's all try to stay calm' tone. She heard Paul's chair squeak as it swivelled and he wandered in.

"Dada!" Jessie called, launching herself over to him and falling at his feet. He picked her up and she played with his shirt collar.

"He's run off? What do you mean? He's in school – how can he run off? How can he just leave school? Is it not secure? How can children just run off? Surely they should…"

"He scaled a fence, Paul. He's jumped over a fence. It's not school's fault."

"Oh, heavens above, so where has he disappeared to this time?" Paul replied, pulling his head back as Jessie tried to tug at his ears.

"Where would he have gone, Paul? He's been so

29

emotional recently. I desperately wanted the new school to go right for him. Things were looking better over the summer. He seemed to be friends with that boy, Tom, and Malika's mum said he'd been much more outgoing when he'd been round there."

"I just don't understand him," Paul said, pulling Jessie's hands down before she tugged one of his earlobes clean off. Thinking this was a fun game, Jessie squealed in delight and made more efforts to get to his ears. "He's getting more and more distant, but let's do the analysis later – we've got to find him. I suppose he could be at the churchyard, but he doesn't even want to go there anymore. Where would a child who is desperately missing their old school go?"

They paused for a moment then looked at each other. Sally reached for her phone.

James was sitting under the familiar cave-like bush, overlooking his old primary school field. The ground was damp and there was a musty smell. He ripped the rest of the pocket off his blazer, tossed it to one side and pulled his knees towards him and rested his chin on them. He needed to text home, but he couldn't face getting his phone out. James knew there would be missed calls from home and a variety of texts from his mum ranging from sadness to anger. A couple more minutes, just a few more solitary minutes before he'd have to face up to the chaos he had no doubt unleashed.

James's stomach tensed. Mrs Barton, his old headteacher, and Mrs Shah were walking across the field towards him. Mrs Barton was wearing the same black skirt, white blouse and black blazer she'd worn as long as James could remember. It was accompanied by a very serious face. Mrs Shah was wearing a beautiful green dress with gold diamond shapes and a beige sari crossed her body. Beyond them, at the other end of the field, was the school building. James could see the lights on in classrooms and children's heads at desks. Through the leaves, he saw Mrs Shah and Mrs Barton say something to each other. Mrs Barton stopped about fifteen metres away. Mrs Shah folded her arms and walked slowly towards the bush. She stopped in front of it and James put his head back on his knees.

"James, are you ok? Do you feel ready to come out?" Mrs Shah spoke softly, and it immediately put him at ease hearing her gentle accent again. "It's ok, James. I understand. I just need to know you're ok."

James couldn't speak. He didn't want Mrs Shah to see him in that state. He felt deeply, cringingly embarrassed, but he couldn't just wander out like everything was fine. Mrs Shah pulled a branch back and James squinted, his eyes adjusting to the light.

"There you are. It's good to see you again, James, although admittedly I didn't think it would be inside a bush! I thought the next time I saw you it would be on a gardening programme on TV. How are your roses doing?"

Earlier in the year, when James had the idea to grow roses for the churchyard, Mrs Shah had helped him, finding some books and offering encouragement when needed. But over the last few weeks, growing roses had been the last thing on James's mind. Mrs Shah pulled some more of the branches to one side, she bent awkwardly and prised herself inside. Ducking down, she sat herself next to James. All he could think about was her beautiful dress – he hoped it wasn't getting dirty because of him. He was also very conscious of what a state he looked; his hair and face were sticky and his uniform was ripped and muddy.

"Is there anything I can do to help, James?" Mrs Shah asked gently.

James pressed the heels of his hands to his eyes until he saw stars.

"I don't think I can go to high school anymore. I just can't do it. I… I want to come back here."

"I see," said Mrs Shah thoughtfully. "Well that's ok, James. You're not going to be the only one who feels like that, I have children come back to visit every year who say the same thing. It's completely normal – you were here for seven years. You're not just going to forget us – I'd be offended if you did! It's very common for me to have this conversation."

James tried to ignore Mrs Barton on the field in front of them. She kept looking at her watch and glancing back at the school building.

"I miss it here." James felt tired and didn't want to be sitting under a bush anymore. He wanted to be at home in bed with the covers pulled over his head.

"It wouldn't feel the same coming back here, James. Try and let what comes come, and let what goes go. There's a Hindu saying, *The whole secret of existence is to try and not have fear*. You proved this year with your roses at the churchyard what you can achieve when you put your mind to it. You might be struggling at the moment because change is difficult, but try to see the opportunities through the difficulties. Good things will come if you open your mind to them. We still think about all the children who leave us, you'll always be part of the school's history."

Mrs Barton was now jangling a bunch of keys loudly in her hand.

"I… I set up a website about the village's history." James wanted to show Mrs Shah he wasn't completely crazy.

"I know you did, James. We've already used it in class for our Year 6 local history topic. It is a wonderful resource. See, you're still a part of our lessons!"

James attempted a smile. He thought back to something Mrs Samuel had once said about her husband, Harry. If you miss something, it means you had a nice time – and those memories then become precious. We should enjoy memories and try not to feel sad about them.

"I'm sorry," he said, feeling guilty – he hated drawing attention to himself and today he'd managed to put himself at the centre of everyone's focus. "I'm sorry you had to come out here because of me. I hope your dress isn't dirty."

"It's fine, James," she replied, smiling at him. "Look, your parents are here. Let's get out of the bush shall we?"

As he struggled out, James saw his parents looking flustered and concerned and Jessie was squirming to get down out of Paul's arms. Paul seemed to be saying something very apologetic to Mrs Barton.

"Jay, Jay?" Jessie called uncertainly and started toddling towards him with her arms stretched towards him.

James picked Jessie up, who clung on to him, and he walked towards his parents.

"James, what…?" Sally began, her voice unusually high-pitched. She was looking him up and down, lines etched in her face.

"I know. I'm sorry," James said.

Sally stepped forward and put her arm around James and Jessie, and hugged them both tight.

"I want to find Mrs Samuel," James whispered through the tangle of arms.

Chapter 7

The week continued with a strange atmosphere at home, with so much being unsaid. School was also weird. James didn't want to go back in, but Sally insisted. There was no one to stay home with him. Sally had to drop Jessie off at nursery then go to work at her new job as an admin assistant in an office. Paul had to go for a meeting at the bank.

James got to school early – preferring to be the first in. He could sit in the classroom on his own and wait for others to drift in, gradually readjusting to a busy classroom rather than walk into one where pupils already were. Mr Fellows had the world's most awkward conversation with him about how he was there for James if he needed him, all he had to do was ask. James wasn't going to ask. On his way to first lesson, Malika bounded up to him and escorted him, glaring at anyone who dared to look at James, never mind snigger or aim a sarcastic comment at him. James went bright red, but this single act helped him get through the morning. Malika had a sixth sense when James needed support and he was relieved and grateful, even if he couldn't tell her.

Of course people were going to be talking about his escape act, James knew that. He doubted anyone would know *where* he went, but just the fact he went anywhere was going to become the week's gossip. Not only was he the strange silent boy, he was now the strange silent boy who had a pear thrown at his head and jumped over a fence. At break-time, James had to go to see the Headteacher, Mrs Denton. Mr Fellows was there too. She also offered sympathy and support, but with a firmer tone than Mr Fellows. She stressed that James must not, under any circumstances, even think about leaving the school premises again and she said that she had nearly phoned the police. As he was leaving the office, Josh, Tom and the other boys were lined up against the opposite wall. They were smirking to each other as the door opened, but quickly stood up straight and stared ahead. Only Tom glanced at James. James felt bitterly betrayed by him. Why didn't he say something and stop it? They were no longer talking, but James thought Tom would at least look out for him. Obviously not.

That weekend, The Big Chat came. James was reading on his bed. Paul, trying to look as relaxed as possible with a mug of tea in his hand, came and sat next to him. Sally had just put Jessie down for a nap and came and leant against the doorframe. There was no escape.

"We get it James, we do. It's a new school. It's a lot to take in. Boys get up to their japes – it's not nice to be on the receiving end of it. It happened to me a few times – some boys put me in a wheelie bin and pushed me around in front of everyone. I had to plaster a big grin on my face like

I was enjoying it. But you can't just run away from school. It's not safe. Anything could happen."

"They threw that stupid pear at my head," James replied, looking at Sally accusingly. "They were laughing. I didn't know what to do."

"I know James and we've spoken to school – what happened to you is completely unacceptable, but I think you have to stop moping. It's very hard to even have a conversation with you at the moment."

James's hackles started to rise. He felt under attack, like *he* was the one who had done something terrible.

"I'm not moping. I just…I'm…"

"Mrs Shah and Mrs Barton had to take time out of their day to help you. You have to deal with things properly, go and talk to your tutor if you feel your temper rising."

"I…I wasn't angry. It wasn't my temper." He jumped off the bed so he was standing in front of Paul feeling ready to explode. "I'm… I'm sick of this. You don't understand anything!"

The tears were welling in his eyes. Paul got up too and stood over James.

"You're not the only one with problems, James. You need to consider that. I'm working all the hours of the day to make my business work. Your mum has had to return to work to try to keep the wolf from the door. You don't even think about that do…"

"Paul! That's enough!" Sally hissed from the doorway.

James turned from Paul, his face on fire, and stormed past Sally.

Chapter 8

James hadn't done this for a while and it felt good – pounding out his anger on the pavements of Hartlewich. He ended up on the bench by the church which overlooked the churchyard and the village beyond. He missed meeting Mrs Samuel here – it had become an important part of his weekend. He went over to Harry's grave. He'd never even met Harry – only seen him in a few of Mrs Samuel's photos, but he *felt* he knew him. There is no way Mrs Samuel would have let the grave get into this state. The grass needed a trim around the base of the gravestone and it needed a good polish. Removing the drooping flowers from the ceramic vase at the base, James decided he would give the grave a proper clean next time just like Mrs Samuel used to. She would never have come without fresh flowers either.

James took an extended route home, earphones plugged in. Aretha Franklin was playing from a playlist on his phone – he called it *Mrs Samuel's 1960s Tunes*. A year previously he had absolutely no interest in music, but after flicking through Mrs Samuel's eclectic record collection, he had been determined to explore these legendary artists. He loved finding new music and it was exciting discovering musicians and bands and realise they had a whole catalogue of songs to explore.

James found himself at the other end of the village to the church. If he went any further, the main road would join the bypass which skirted the village. The houses here were much bigger than James's house, with longer drives and large front gardens. James turned and returned the way he had come, deciding to head back home. Flicking through the tracks on his playlist, a bustle of activity caught his attention and made him glance over to the other side of the road. A thick hedge obscured most of what lay behind it, but between two gate posts a red brick building was visible. It had the look of a characterless modern office block, with identical windows in rows along the length of the building and a sliding door entrance in the middle. There was a small gravel car park in front. James hadn't paid any attention to the building in the past – it was mostly hidden from view. A sign, covered in moss, rose above the hedge – 'The Grange Manor Care Home'. At least the name sounded grand.

An ambulance was parked outside the building. It wasn't one of the emergency ambulances that go whizzing past with lights flashing, it was more like a mini-bus which transported people back and to for appointments. James saw two ambulance staff at the back in high-vis jackets, raising a ramp to the back doors of the vehicle. Another member of staff pushed a wheelchair from inside the ambulance to the ramp. James was just about to turn back to his playlist when he spotted a familiar bobble hat on the patient's head, and heard an even more familiar voice – Mrs Samuel! It was Mrs Samuel being lowered on the ramp. Clearly indignant about something, she was reprimanding the staff and wafting her hand at them. She was wheeled towards the building still grumbling as the door slid open and then closed shut behind them. James stared in disbelief at a silent car park.

"Why didn't John Samuel tell us where she was?" James said to Sally when he returned home. She was folding the village newsletter, ready to put through people's letterboxes later that day.

"I don't know, love," Sally replied, relieved that the earlier argument seemed to have been forgotten. "Some people don't like others involved in their lives. Maybe

he's just very private. Not everyone is friendly with people they don't know very well. Who knows?"

"I'd like to visit her, go up there and see her. I'm sure she'd want visitors. We don't even know what that place is like. She'll be missing home."

"She was struggling, James. I'm sure it'll be the best place for her. She'll be well looked after."

"I only wrote to John Samuel to get him involved in her life, not so he could remove her from her home and stick her in a place like that," James said, exasperated.

"Listen, I'll contact him again and ask if you can go – so you can see for yourself where she is staying. I know he *saw* my other message, maybe he meant to reply and forgot. I can only try, but you have to accept if he doesn't want you…"

The doorbell rang and Paul emerged from 'the cupboard'.

"Who on earth is that? I've got stuff to do," he said, tucking his shirt in and running a hand through his hair.

"The house is in a state. Don't let them in whoever it is," said Sally, looking at the stacks of newsletters on the table.

James didn't like anything unexpected. Unless it was his mum or dad, he wouldn't even answer his phone if it rang because he hadn't had time to prepare for the conversation. He certainly didn't like people turning up at the house unannounced.

Sally went to answer the door, stopping to check herself in the mirror.

"Jeremy! Denise! Lewis! What a… lovely surprise!"

James screwed up his face and groaned to himself.

"Jeremy, nice to see you. If only there was some kind of technology where you could send a message to warn people you're on your way," said Paul, joining Sally at the door.

"Very funny, very funny. Just passing by on the way to the match and thought I'd say hello to my favourite brother and his lovely missus. Out is she?" Jeremy replied, winking at Sally and laughing loudly at his own joke.

Jeremy didn't wait to be invited in, barging past Paul and Sally. Uncle Jeremy, Auntie Denise and Lewis were all wearing matching football shirts with their own names printed on the back. They were larger-than-life characters with very little filter – if they thought it, they said it. The one saving grace was that they didn't care if anyone replied to them or not – they didn't listen anyway.

"Here he is!" boomed Uncle Jeremy, entering the kitchen. "My favourite nephew in Hartlewich."

Uncle Jeremy cracked this joke every time he saw James, and James had to force a smile each time knowing he was Uncle Jeremy's *only* nephew in Hartlewich. Uncle Jeremy ruffled James's hair roughly. James hated his fringe being touched.

"Heard you've been practising the high jump over the school fence. Good lad! I bunked off school a few times myself," Uncle Jeremy continued.

"Jeremy, leave the poor boy alone, he's had a tough time, haven't you James? It's not easy settling into a new school, especially when you're as painfully shy as James is," said Auntie Denise, joining them in the kitchen.

"I can't wait to get out of primary school and be with the big lads. My teacher says I'm outgrowing primary school and I'm ready to move up," said Lewis, who was a year younger than James.

"*They're* ready for you to move up, more like!" shouted Uncle Jeremy. Auntie Denise cackled.

"What's this? Got yourself a paper round now, Sally?" said Uncle Jeremy, chuckling at the newsletters.

"Oh, you know, I might as well put my Saturday afternoon to good use. It keeps me fit and it's a bit of extra pocket money for us."

"Our pocket money comes from our investment portfolios. That must take you hours," said Auntie Denise, eyeing the newsletters in disgust. She walked over to the kettle, her high heels clicking on the floor and flicked the kettle on. "What do you have to do to get a drink round here? I'm parched and we need to leave for the football soon. Jeremy's got us an executive box, haven't you Jeremy?"

After Jeremy, Denise and Lewis had departed and calm had resumed, James folded the remaining newsletters while Sally cooked lunch. Sally was whisking eggs in a jug when her phone pinged.

"James," Sally said, picking up her phone and hesitating, "he says you can go. John Samuel, he's replied and says you can go to see his mum."

James sensed something in her tone.

"What did he say? When should I go?" James asked. For a second, he thought it might be better if he just forgot the whole thing. James often found the easy option was not to go to new places, where he would have to interact with people. It became a vicious cycle for him. He hated going places because of his social anxieties, but he found it hard to go to places because he *didn't* go to places.

"He just said it would be… nice if you went. He says she would enjoy the company and she'd like to see you." She finally smiled at him and walked over and put her arm around him. "Will you be ok with this, love?"

She knew James struggled doing anything different and it would play on his mind.

"Did he really say that? I wonder why he hasn't been in touch before?" James asked.

"I don't know love, maybe he's been away. Why don't you go tomorrow afternoon? I'll check with Grange Manor. Maybe someone will take you up to Mrs Samuel's room."

Chapter 9

James had absolutely no idea what to expect from the care home. For some reason he imagined a large, long room with lots of old-fashioned hospital beds along each side. Old people would be propped up on pillows shouting to each other across the room about the good old days. There would be no-nonsense matronly-type nurses with crisp blue uniforms and an air of discipline who would keep things running smoothly.

"You mean you're not coming in with me?" James asked Sally.

"You don't need me there. She's your friend and they won't want lots of people wandering around the home. I'll drive you up there and maybe you could walk back when you're ready?"

James spent Sunday morning pacing around the house. He played with Jessie – pretending to throw a squishy ball, but hiding it in his hands and looking around dramatically at where the ball could have gone. Jessie was giggling uncontrollably like this was the funniest thing she had ever seen: "Ball Jay, Jay. Ball!"

That afternoon, Sally drove him to the top of the village and pulled into the gravel car park. There were only a couple of other cars there.

"Do a short visit today, just to get used to it and see what's what. Next time you might feel a bit more confident," Sally said, and reached over and squeezed James's hand.

James undid his seat belt and looked over his shoulder towards the building. There was no sign of anyone around.

"Will there be someone there at the door?" James asked.

"You probably need to knock or ring. Go on. You'll be fine."

"Make sure you wait here for a few minutes," James replied. If he had to get out of there, at least his mum would be waiting for a quick getaway.

James opened the car door and crept across the stones, each crunch of his footsteps sounded so loud. When he got to the block paving area outside the building, the large glass door in front of him jerked and slid open with a whirring sound. There was a small area with nothing but a wooden table to the right. On top was a vase of dusty fake flowers, a book with a pen attached on a piece of string and some hand sanitiser. Tacked to the wall was a laminated sign which was curling at the corners, telling visitors to sign in. Doing as he was told, James wrote his name, the time and who he was visiting. He squirted the sanitiser and rubbed it in as he contemplated what to do next. In front of him was another sliding door – this one stayed firmly shut. James weighed it up, stepped backwards, then forwards again in the hope there had been some kind of mistake and it had forgotten to slide open. Noticing a bell to his left, he gave it a press. There was no sound, so he kept pressing. Still nothing. No one came and the door stayed resolutely shut. This did nothing to ease James's nerves. He decided that the best course of action was to keep his finger on the bell for a while then run back to the car if no one came. Just as he was about to give up, the shadowy figure of a person appeared on the other side of the glass. They reached up and pressed a button and the door slid open. James sprang back and stood upright with his hands by his sides like he had been caught doing something wrong.

The door revealed the smiling face of a young lady. She wore a bright blue tunic which *did* look a little bit like a nurse's uniform, and black trousers. She had brown hair, brown eyes and dimples in her cheeks which made her look friendly.

"Ahhh you must be James," she said in an Irish accent. "There's not many twelve year olds call by here on a Sunday afternoon. Just so you know, James, you can't hear the bell when you press it, but the rest of the care home can. We've had seven complaints from residents because you've woken them from their afternoon naps."

James gulped. "Oh, gosh. I'm… I'm so sorry."

The lady giggled. "I'm only joking. We *can* hear the bell though – I need to make a sign really, to tell people they only need to press it once. I've just taken over as manager, it's not really been my first priority – I'll get round to it though! My name's Laura, come on through."

James stepped through the sliding doors. There was a lift straight ahead with a staircase to the right of it. To his left were some brown double doors and through the glass James could see what looked like a large lounge, with chairs dotted around. The chairs didn't look like normal house chairs, they were taller and higher. A couple of residents were reading books. Another had her head on her hand and looked like she was nodding off. An old gentleman was being brought a cup of tea by another lady in a blue tunic and they chatted happily as she placed the cup in his hand.

"The residents had a keep-fit session this morning and the lady who ran it was full of beans. I think she forgot the average age of her class was eighty. She's tired them all out!" Laura laughed. "Ahh, Cliff. Would you mind taking this young man up to Julia Samuel's room, she's your floor isn't she?"

A tall gentleman with a slight stoop was walking towards them.

"No problem, Laura. No problem at all. Let's take the stairs – the lift's for the old 'uns." He had a warm, deep voice with a slight Caribbean accent. He was wearing a burgundy tunic, with black trousers and a pair of white trainers on his feet. He was completely bald and had gold reading glasses hanging from a chain round his neck. James quickly calculated that he was probably in his mid-fifties. He walked slowly and although he didn't smile, he had a twinkle in his eyes and James immediately sensed patience and kindness. James had a 'people radar' and it rarely let him down; he picked up on tiny clues about someone's character very quickly.

Cliff plodded upwards, wafting his hand to indicate that James should follow.

"This your first time here visiting your grandma?" Cliff asked, not looking back.

James coughed out a 'yes'. He couldn't even begin to explain Mrs Samuel wasn't actually his grandma or relay how he did actually did know her. When they got to the top of the stairs, they were in the middle of a long corridor. The carpet was a speckled red colour and the walls were beige, with pictures of flowers and landscapes on them. Along each wall there was a hand rail running the length of the corridor. Every few metres along the wall there was a doorway.

'We're this way," said Cliff, turning right. "She'll be pleased to see you. She's quite a character is Julia, keeps us on our toes that's for sure. The residents can sometimes take a few weeks to settle in. It can be a shock to them suddenly losing their independence, but she's made herself right at home."

Walking down the centre of the corridor, James tried to keep his eyes straight but he couldn't help glancing in some of the rooms either side. Each room was exactly the same – small, with a bed along the wall. There was a chair beneath the window, a chest of drawers and another door to the left of the main door which James presumed was a little bathroom. In some rooms, an older person was sitting in the high armchair underneath the window at the end of the room. Some were reading; others were watching the TV on the wall; some were staring out of the doorway in front of them. A few of them waved and called a 'hello' as James passed. Cliff was now a few metres ahead and James did a little quick step to try and catch up. Passing one of the rooms, James heard a voice call out.

"Hey, lad. Here! Good morning!"

James hesitated. Cliff hadn't turned round, but he didn't want to appear rude and ignore the man.

Stopping, James took a few paces back and stood at the man's door. He was impeccably turned out with a tweed suit, pocket watch and porkpie hat on his head.

"Ahh there you are lad, have you got my papers to sign? They're supposed to be here today. Where are they?" He spoke in a cut-glass accent.

James stared blankly at the man. "I… erm… papers?"

James felt the man's glare. He rubbed his arm and looked up the corridor. Where had Cliff gone?

"Those papers are important lad, they need signing before midday. Get Janice for me, she'll get to the bottom of it."

"Janice?" James's voice quivered.

"Ahh, you've met Mr Adamson." Cliff reappeared next to James. "All ok, Mr Adamson?"

Mr Adamson's tone softened a little, "I'm still waiting on those papers, Cliff. There seems to be a hold up – I could really do with them by midday, if you could look into it old chap?"

"Right away, Mr Adamson." Cliff turned and winked at James. "Come on, Mrs Samuel is waiting. We'll be seeing you, Mr Adamson."

Mr Adamson looked slightly happier but lifted his pocket watch to check the time.

"Mr Adamson used to be a solicitor before he retired. If he gets too agitated about his papers, we sometimes take him some pretend ones, just so he has something to sign. We have to tie them up in pink ribbon – a tradition in the legal world, apparently. You learn all sorts here," Cliff chuckled, as James followed him. "He might get a bit confused sometimes, but he's still got a sharp legal brain, I can tell you. Under this roof we've got ex-police chiefs, teachers, doctors, musicians and artists. People walk past this place and ignore it, but there's enough talent, knowledge and experience under this roof to fill an encyclopaedia. It'd be better than any internet and more interesting too."

James looked dubiously either side at the old people in their rooms.

"The *really* interesting ones have lived unremarkable lives. The people who have been refuse collectors, secretaries, shop workers, or not worked at all but brought up a family. You talk to them, and *they're* the ones with the stories to tell. You realise they *are* remarkable. Ahh here we are," Cliff said at the end of the corridor, "Julia Samuel's room. Mrs Samuel."

Cliff gestured his arm to the open doorway on the left. James hesitated, before rounding the corner. In front of him was Mrs Samuel. She was sitting in the chair under the window like many of the other residents were. She looked tiny in the tall chair, but James was relieved to see her looking healthier than the last time he saw her. She'd put on a bit of weight and her clothes were matching. She was wearing a blue skirt, white blouse and cardigan – it was the first time James had seen her wearing clothes that looked like they had been chosen with some thought. Her glasses looked cleaner, like they were getting a regular polish. She was clearly doing well without the confusion of having to organise her life and remember if she had paid the gas bill or got the shopping in, or eaten. The pen and key tied around her neck with grubby string had gone.

Kicking himself for not pre-planning some small-talk topics of conversation, James didn't know what to say.

"Ok, Mrs Samuel?" Cliff asked. "James is here. Sit down, James. I'll be back in a minute to see how you're getting on."

Mrs Samuel took a moment to consider James and he could see her mind rewinding, trying to search for him from within her memory. Then her face brightened.

"Don't just stand there gawping at me like I'm an ancient exhibit in a museum, son. Sit down, for heaven's sake. They said you were coming. I said to them, well it's about time! He's not bothered much so far," she chortled.

"I'm sorry, I… I didn't know where you were," James stammered, feeling hurt.

"Of course you didn't, son. I'm just pulling your leg. I've told them all about you, growing all those roses for the gravestones in the churchyard."

James perched down on the edge of the bed next to Mrs Samuel. He looked around the room and relaxed a little.

"Do you like it? Here I mean, in the care home. Do you like it?" James asked.

"I'm getting used to it, son. It's like being a child again, being told what to do and when to do it. But it's a roof over my head and for that I should be thankful. We get three meals a day, not like my fresh home cooked meals but three meals nonetheless," Mrs Samuels sniffed.

Remembering Mrs Samuel's kitchen, the bare cupboards and empty fridge, James was just relieved she was being well fed.

Cliff reappeared with a jug of water and placed it on the bedside table next to Mrs Samuel's chair. Leaning closer to James, she whispered, "They won't give me my aspirin though. My joints are giving me some gip, but will they let me have my painkillers? No they will not."

Cliff picked up a used cup and replaced it with a fresh one and smiled. "Now Julia, we've had this conversation. You had your aspirin two hours ago, you can't have more for at least another couple of hours. Don't go telling this young man we're not looking after you."

Mrs Samuel shook her head at James when Cliff turned his back to straighten some of the knick-knacks on top of the chest of drawers, to confirm this great conspiracy. On the wall, there were a number of pictures of John and Harry, and in the middle of them was the picture from Mrs Samuel's hallway of her and Harry when they were a young couple.

"It's important our residents have as many pictures as possible around the room," said Cliff, noticing James looking at them. "It helps keep their memories alive. It's important for staff too – gives us something to talk about with the residents and it shows us behind each old person is a life lived, and someone who was young once just like us.

Well, not like me. I'll need to book my room in this place myself in a few years, but you know what I mean, James!"

James and Mrs Samuel chatted for a while. James talked about school, the village and the churchyard. He reminded Mrs Samuel about the website he'd set up for the Hartlewich Historical Society and showed her on his phone. Mrs Samuel looked pleased but James wasn't sure she understood what a website was. The society was something Mrs Samuel had run for years until she felt too old for the responsibility – no one had offered to take it over. Mrs Samuel leaned forward again and took James's hand, frowning.

"I don't get to go to the churchyard any more, son. I hope Harry's grave isn't all overgrown. They won't let me out of here to check. The only way I can go is if John comes and takes me but I've not seen him for a while."

"I'll… I'll keep an eye on it. I'll make sure it's ok. I promise," said James.

She sat back again, deep in thought. They fell into a companionable silence and James tinkered on his phone and sent his mum a text to say he was ok. When he looked up Mrs Samuel's eyes were heavy and she was dozing off.

Cliff bobbed back in, "Ahh we finally get some peace," he joked. "We need to invite the keep-fit lady more often if it sends them all to sleep. Today has been a good day for Mrs Samuel, James."

James wasn't quite sure if Cliff meant because of the keep-fit, or because he had been to see her or for some other reason, but he felt pleased that the visit was done and Mrs Samuel was her usual self.

"Don't forget to write your name in her book," Cliff said, pointing to the top of the chest of drawers. It reminds her who has been and gives us something else to talk to her about."

James got up and turned to the first page, which was blank. He wrote his name and the date and a little comment saying it had been nice to see her.

"She keeps talking about a song. She's driving us mad going on about it," Cliff continued, showing James out.

"She…she really likes music," said James. "The Beatles, Elvis and lots of others. I listen to them now too. Her wedding dance was to Elvis."

"Ahh lovely, but I don't think it's Elvis or The Beatles. She gets quite worked up about it. A song that meant a lot to her and she wants to listen to it. No doubt it will come to her. Anyway young James, we shall see you again I'm sure."

Chapter 10

If there was one thing James liked to do, it was establishing a routine. So at 2pm, every Saturday afternoon, he would make his way to the end of the village and visit Mrs Samuel at Grange Manor. Sometimes she would be full of life and chatting away, but other times she would sit quietly and conversation would be scarce. James would show Mrs Samuel photos on his phone he had taken of Harold's gravestone. She'd always have a comment to make.

"Grass is looking a bit overgrown, might need a bit of a trim next time you go. Is that a smudge on the marble near the engraving? Give that a polish next time, son."

Mrs Samuel used to carry the contents of a cleaning cupboard around in the basket on her walker, calling it her magic bag.

"That blessed bird," she said, pointing to the little ornament she had taped to the top of the gravestone to make sure she could find the grave. "Never could get it to stay upright!"

James began to feel a bit more comfortable around the care home and would smile and offer a little wave to the residents who called to him. Rather than speeding past Mr Adamson's room when he shouted out for his papers, James would reply.

"I think they might be coming later, Mr Adamson."

One afternoon, James rounded the doorway into Mrs Samuel's room and Cliff was perched next to her, holding his phone. A cable led from the phone to a pair of earphones plugged into Mrs Samuel's ears and her face was a picture of impish delight.

"Ahh James, good afternoon," Cliff said in his Caribbean drawl. He pressed something and Mrs Samuel bopped her head along in time. "Now, this lady here keeps going on about all this music she listened to in the 1960s. She keeps asking about one song in particular and I've not been able to help her there, so what I thought I'd do is offer her some education on some real music – reggae! We've had a few minutes of the genius that is Bob Marley! You heard of him, James?"

James shook his head in bemusement at them.

"That's a real shame, James. You must add him to your playlist! I grew up listening to reggae, James. My parents came here on a boat from Jamaica in the 1950s with nothing but a suitcase full of clothes and a few reggae records. They worked night and day doing jobs no one wanted just to scrape a living, not that anyone ever thanked them. They wanted to pay to bring more family over but they never earned enough, and then they had me and my brother and sisters. I've still got family back there, I'd love to go and see them one day. There's not much chance of that, more's the pity. I've managed to save a bit over the years, but not enough."

"He's not bad, this Rob Barley," Mrs Samuel shouted over the music playing in her ears, "but I still love The Beatles and my Elvis."

Cliff mock-tutted and shook his head.

"Today is a good day James," he said as he left the room. "Talk to her. Listen to her. Ask her things."

James and Mrs Samuel made small talk for a while. James mentioned how he uploaded blogs about the village's history on his website and then spent considerable time explaining what a blog actually was.

"It's all beyond my imagination, son, all this technology. We didn't even have a TV when I was a child, now everyone has the world at their fingertips on a tiny contraption that fits in their pocket. We used to watch all the top music groups in the 1960s, me and my friends. We went to all the local venues – the Cavern, the Memorial Hall, Mersey View, Parr Hall and the Royalty Theatre. They were called 'Dances' in those days and we saw all the local groups like The Beatles and Gerry and the Pacemakers. Some big American stars came over too, like Roy Orbison. There wouldn't just be one group to watch, there'd be lots of them playing, one after the other during the evening. The 'top of the bill' would come on last. But there wasn't the internet, there weren't even computers, so we only found out about the dances in the local newspapers each week, or if we saw a poster up in town. Somehow everybody knew what was on each week. We had some good times and we got quite friendly with some of these groups. They'd sign our autograph books and chat to us. In return, when they started playing we would stand in front of the stage and dance and scream and everyone would wonder who this really popular band was! I've still got that autograph book somewhere – not seen it for years. John must have it now. I hope he's looking after it."

Laura brought a cup of tea and plumped the cushion Mrs Samuel was leaning on. A few sips seemed to recharge her memories further. She talked about Harry and how he'd had a job at the local works for most of his life. She told James how Harry and John made go-karts out of wood and a treehouse. Harry hadn't passed the 11+ exam so had gone to a technical school – the result was that he could turn his hand to almost anything around the house. Mrs Samuel told James about the time Harry had been furious with John for scrumping apples from a garden on the street, and James couldn't imagine anyone these days finding an apple so exciting they'd risk getting into trouble for stealing one.

"It was a big deal to get taken on at the works, it was what all the local lads wanted. Harry joined at sixteen and stayed there fifty years," Mrs Samuel said. "It wasn't well paid by any means and it was hard labour, but it was a job for life and men in those days wanted to be able to provide security for their family. Harry was keen for John to get a job there too, just like *he* had followed in his own father's footsteps. John had other ideas – computers. All that new-fangled technology was starting to take off, and John got himself a computer qualification and never looked back. Broke Harry's heart, it did. It was a world he didn't understand. Who could blame John though? Manufacturing industries were dying and the works were bulldozed soon after Harry retired. John now has his own business working for hospitals doing all their computer wizardry. I don't understand it all really but it's fair to say he's made something of himself. Harry was proud, I know he was, but like lots of men of his generation, he struggled to say it."

James was absorbing everything Mrs Samuel said, just like he used to. He looked at his watch and realised he'd been sitting there for nearly two hours and got up to leave.

"Well that's your next few blags sorted then. I've given you lots of history there, son. No one remembers old codgers like me, stuck in this home. It's nice to have someone interested for a change," said Mrs Samuel as he left.

"Blogs, erm, they're blogs," James said, trying not to smile.

Mrs Samuel laughed, "I told you it was all beyond me, son."

But she was right, and James got straight down to work on his next blog that night.

Chapter 11

It was the tradition at James's high school that the Year 7s had the option to walk to church on the afternoon they broke up for the December holidays to take part in a festive service. It felt strange walking across the Village Hall car park, through the lychgate and up the churchyard path to the front porch of the church with lots of other people. This was usually a solitary activity for James. Spirits were high and children were laughing, play fighting and pushing each other onto the grass. James was at the back of the line. He saw Malika pull someone back onto the path and point at the grave the girl had been standing on. She did it with a smile and such an easy manner, James could see why everyone respected her so much. The girl she had reprimanded draped an arm round Malika's back and they walked up the path giggling together. James couldn't imagine ever having a social interaction like that. The pupils lined up to enter the church next to the yew tree outside the porch door. The tree was covered in twinkling lights and they could hear organ music from inside the church.

Reverend Varga delivered the festive service. James hadn't seen her since before the summer holidays. He loved listening to her warm and melodic Eastern European accent. Discussing the joy of giving, she was fighting a losing battle against the buoyant mood of over two-hundred twelve year olds packed into a church, who had kept a lid on their excitement all week but were now only an hour away from breaking up for the end of term. Some were kicking each other beneath the pews or flicking the ears of those in front. James hated situations like this and felt tense in the rowdy atmosphere. He was relieved that he was sitting on the back pew with no one to do anything to him from behind. Some of the teachers sitting at the end of the rows were ignoring the behaviour and pretending to find Reverend Varga's sermon far too interesting to notice, while some were discreetly trying in vain to catch a pupil's eye to shush them.

The best part of the service by a mile was Malika singing a gospel version of 'Silent Night'. James loved this carol, and Malika's voice filled the church and made the hairs on the back of James's neck stand on end. It was the only point of the service when everyone was paying attention to what was going on – every single pair of eyes were on Malika. She was an amazing singer. After some readings, all the pupils sang 'O Come All Ye Faithful' which wasn't quite as impressive. It remained almost in tune until the third 'O come, let us adore Him' at the end of each chorus, where all control was lost.

Towards the end of the service, a head bobbed forward out of the row of children sitting further up the pew to James. It was Malika, with her usual sparkling grin. She seemed to be mouthing something in his direction. At first James ignored her, certain it couldn't be him she was attempting to talk to. He didn't want to embarrass himself by acknowledging her and then realise it was someone behind him she was trying to catch the eye of. James wanted to crawl under a stone when things like that happened, so he kept his eyes fixed on the front of the church just in case. Malika was now doing a wild double-handed wave and James couldn't ignore her anymore. She tried again and James shrugged, unsure what she was saying. Exaggerating the words, she mouthed it again slowly:

"Can…I…walk…home…with…you?"

One of the perks of the Christmas service was that you were allowed to walk home directly from the church if you lived nearby. James nodded, and the initial feeling of warmth he felt immediately gave way to worrying whether the talking part of his brain was going to play ball.

When the service finished and the children shuffled out, James held back to avoid the crush. He was convinced Malika wouldn't have waited and maybe part of him hoped she hadn't, but she was there at the entrance near the main road. She was chatting to a couple of girls, who looked James up and down as he approached, then turned on their heels and walked off in the other direction, whispering to each other.

"Hey James, let's go, shall we?" Malika said. Behind them they heard a loud 'woooo' and whistling from the group of boys Tom was standing with. Josh let out an exaggerated laugh.

"Jealous *you* haven't got my company home?" Malika called back. "Come on, James." She pulled his coat sleeve to more jeers, and they made their way down the main road towards the centre of the village.

Malika chatted non-stop about the church service and her plans for the two-week break, and her annoying little brother and just about anything that came to her mind. This was why James found it easier to spend time with Malika than anyone else. It didn't matter if he struggled to talk; it didn't matter that he didn't always answer when she spoke. Malika accepted it was who he was. He still wished more than anything that he could chat back in the same way, but literally nothing came to his mind. If it did, he couldn't get it out of his mouth quick enough anyway.

They walked past the village shops; people were

wrapped up in scarves, gloves and hats and hurrying between the shops. The sky above them was a dark, golden grey.

"It's starting to snow, James!" Malika cried, and James couldn't help smiling at her endearing excitement.

By the time they turned off the main road into the deserted side street that led to James's house, the snow was falling heavier and starting to leave a thin layer on the ground. Streetlights sprang on around them, illuminating circles of glittery yellow on the pavement making James feel like he was on a magical movie set.

"Come on!" called Malika, grabbing James's hand. She ran and skidded along the ground in the snow and James did the same. They did it again, but this time Malika over-skidded, her legs shot forwards from underneath her and she fell to the ground with a thump. She sat for a moment, still holding James's hand from the floor. Malika started shaking and, for a horrifying moment, James thought she was crying and he was going to have to provide some kind of comfort. Then she burst out laughing and James laughed too, more in relief than anything.

Rubbing away the snow with a coat sleeve pulled over her hand, Malika manoeuvred herself up onto the curb and perched there. She pulled her hood over her head and James did the same.

"Your song was good. You're… you're a great singer," said James, emboldened by the security of the hood hiding half of his face.

"Thanks, James!" Malika replied, sounding delighted. "I really want to sing more. Maybe have some singing lessons, but my parents don't have much spare time to take me to a teacher. I'd love the chance to sing at different places, like proper gigs."

With the ice broken, Malika turned and looked straight at James.

"Why are you so quiet, James? Is there something wrong with you?" James was stung by the bluntness of her question which Malika noticed and immediately responded to. "I don't mean that in a horrible way, silly. It doesn't bother me. It's just sometimes people ask me and I don't really know what to say. I know you're shy but maybe I could help people understand."

If anyone else was having this conversation with him, James would be dying inside. Getting defensive and annoyed, he'd shut up shop completely and maybe storm off. He trusted Malika. She was so genuine and lacking in judgement, James knew she was coming from a good place. He flicked his fringe from his face.

"I don't know. I just find things hard – hard with people. Life is easier on my own. It's less stressful. The less I'm around people, the less I have to worry about being around people, if you know what I mean. They used to try and find something wrong with me, but I don't know. The way my mind works, it's… it's like my thoughts are books on a massive bookcase. Trying to search for the right book quickly enough to have a conversation is almost impossible. Then I panic because I can't find the book. It's like all the books are tipped on the floor and I'm trying to find the right one at the bottom of the pile. So I stay silent and don't even bother looking for the book."

Malika thought about this then burst out laughing, "Wow, that's a long way of saying you're *really* shy, James!"

James smiled too. "Even if I manage to speak to someone, I… I then go home and replay the conversation in my head for hours and get really embarrassed by everything I did manage to say. It's hard to understand, especially when *you're* so confident."

"I might look super-confident to you, but I'm not. Not really," Malika replied. "I go home and worry. I worry what I look like. I worry about being taller than the other girls. It's not easy being me all the time either. I act confident and outgoing, so people expect me to be *always* confident and outgoing. That can be tiring too!"

James looked at her in disbelief. He would give anything for even a pinch of Malika's personality

"I can't help but feel I stand out in a school full of mostly white children, in a village of mostly white people. I often feel different," Malika continued. "My mum and dad always drill into me to be proud of who I am and to be myself, to enjoy life and be positive. My dad says he's had to fight to get to where he is. I try not to worry about what people think, but it's hard sometimes. I guess I just act a role better than you. But I bet you learn to do that as you get older, when you realise that you're…"

A car turned into the road, its headlights dazzling them and lighting up the flurry of snow. Malika stood up and brushed down her skirt.

"Come on James, it's absolutely freezing, we'll look like two snow people if we stay here any longer."

She linked arms with him and they walked in silence, leaving two sets of footprints together in the snow.

Chapter 12

"Why *do* we have to go to Uncle Jeremy and Auntie Denise's on Christmas Day?"

James was standing at the door to the living room, his hands in his hoodie pockets. Typing away at his laptop on the settee, Paul was mumbling about having to reply to emails on Christmas Eve. Sally was sitting on the carpet showing Jessie the snow globe she had been trying to reach from the mantelpiece for the last two weeks. Each time Sally turned the snow globe, Jessie shrieked and pressed it to her eyes.

"It's only one day, love. It's not fair if they have to come to us *every* year, is it?" Sally replied.

"But it's *Christmas Day*," James continued. He felt comfortable in his *own* home. He found going to other people's houses overwhelming – having to follow someone else's routine. James liked his own family's traditions. What he always loved about Christmas was being cosseted up in his own home on Christmas Eve and being able to shut the door to the world. It was one of the few times of the year where there was no essential reason to leave the home. James loved that. And Jeremy and Denise were so loud. Lovely, but loud.

Paul looked up from his laptop with a frown. "What's this? James you're not going on about Christmas Day *again,* are you? We're going and that's it, you need to get on with it."

James gulped against a lump in his throat.

"I wanted to go and see Mrs Samuel too. I wanted to go tomorrow – just for a while." His voice wobbled.

Paul placed his laptop down on the settee next to him. James could see there was a spreadsheet with lots of numbers on the screen, many of them highlighted in red.

"I know James, but you can go on Boxing Day – she'll still appreciate that. Jeremy and Denise are *our* family, they've been a big support to us recently. Mrs Samuel has her own family who will be visiting her, I'm sure. Like your mum says, it's only one day and next year Christmas will be back at ours."

James turned for the stairs. He stopped and returned to the lounge doorway.

"Can I go now? To Mrs Samuel, I mean. Grange Manor. Just nip for an hour?"

"Oh James, it's Christmas Eve," Paul said. "We've got a little Christmas Eve box for Jessie, just like we did with you when you were little. We were going to give it to her soon. It's starting to get dark." Paul looked at Sally for back up, but she made a sympathetic face which made him sigh.

"Ok then, but don't be long," he said in a resigned tone. "You want a lift?"

James was already at the hall cupboard getting his coat, hat and gloves.

"It's ok, I'll walk. It's not too cold. It won't take me long."

"Text us when you get there and again when you're leaving," called Sally.

Hurrying down the drive, James turned back and tingled as he saw the homely glow of the living room, with Sally and Paul playing with Jessie beside the Christmas tree.

It was only a twenty-minute walk to the care home. At the main road, he paused. Pulling off a glove, James reached into his pocket. He pulled out a crinkled five pound note and a few coins and totted up how much he had. Instead of going left towards the care home, James turned right and headed for the village shops. They had all closed early except for the convenience store. The shelves had been stripped bare by shoppers picking up last-minute presents or items for their Christmas lunch they'd forgotten to get on their 'big shop'. James's money wouldn't stretch far, but he managed to buy the last two boxes of chocolates on the shelf.

When he arrived, each window of Grange Manor was illuminated in the late afternoon gloom. Apart from the fact that it had gone dark so early, it could have been any day of the year. James pressed the bell once and waited. Eventually Laura came to the door, complete with a Santa hat and a cheery smile. She let him in and the cosy warmth hit him. He could hear the muffled sound of Christmas music and laughter.

"Hello, James. Merry Christmas, it's lovely to see you! Mrs Samuel is in the residents lounge this afternoon, in fact everyone is. Do you want us to bring her out?"

"I've got her a present," he held the chocolates forward. "The... the other box is for you – all the staff. For Christmas. To share. Just to say, erm, happy Christmas."

Handing over the chocolates, James blushed, feeling embarrassed by the modest size of the box.

"That's very kind, James! I'll pop them in the staff room, everyone will be so grateful. Now shall we get Mrs Samuel? Come on."

James followed Laura towards the double doors of the lounge where a Christmas song was playing and they both stood for a moment, watching. And you know what? It was the loveliest, most heart-warming thing James had ever seen. He'd watched sentimental programmes on TV which were accompanied by a strings or piano soundtrack and were designed to bring a tear to the eye, but this was real and right in front of him. The residents were gathered in a group, some sitting in the tall chairs, some in wheelchairs, a few standing with sticks. They were draped in tinsel and a couple of residents were waving it like scarves at a football match. Even Mr Adamson had a pair of reindeer ears on his head and was tapping his leg with his hand. Staff were gathered around them all, conducting the singing to 'Rockin' Around the Christmas Tree'. At the end of the song there was a big finish and everyone cheered and clapped. There was a little community of happiness, kindness and camaraderie inside this building which looked like a budget hotel, hidden away from the main road behind a thick hedge. No one else would know it was happening. The older generation who had contributed so much to society and had so many stories to tell; and the staff, away from their own families to be working there on Christmas Eve.

Cliff was manning the CD player.

"The next one's for you, Julia," he called above the merriment in his lilting accent.

The first few bars of an Elvis' 'Blue Christmas' started to play and James saw Mrs Samuel smiling from ear to ear as Cliff went over and crouched beside her.

"No, no don't," James said to Laura as she put her hand on the door. "I mean, don't get her. You don't need to. She loves Elvis. Can you give her my present later?"

"I'll do that, James. I'll tell her you came and Cliff will write it in her book."

"Can… can you say thank you to Cliff. For, for… you know…" James looked over again without finishing his sentence. Cliff was mouthing the words to the song, pretending to be Elvis, which made Mrs Samuel laugh. "Oh, and happy Christmas, will you tell him I said happy Christmas?"

"I *do* know, James, and I will tell him. Happy Christmas to you too."

Chapter 13

On Christmas Day, James, Sally and Paul were up early. They had no choice, Jessie rarely slept later than 6am anyway. James opened his stocking in his pyjamas and they had a leisurely breakfast.

"James, do you fancy wearing something smarter today?" Sally asked tentatively, knowing he didn't. "There's some nice trousers in your cupboard, with the blue shirt that's hanging up. Nothing too outlandish, but you'll look lovely."

James didn't argue. He'd felt the tension in the house recently and wanted, *needed*, Christmas to be relaxed and happy.

When they arrived at Uncle Jeremy and Auntie Denise's house, the pair of them were wearing matching jumpers – something they did every year. This year's choice of knitwear had a snowman on the front with a long sticking-out carrot for a nose which Paul snorted at. Uncle Jeremy was a salesperson at the huge car supermarket up the road. James's cousin, Lewis, was a mini-version of Jeremy and would ask the most excruciating questions without any appreciation of the embarrassment they might cause. In short, Jeremy, Denise and Lewis were James's worst nightmare, but they also had hearts of gold. James's grandma and grandad were there too; they hugged and he felt happy. The thought of something was often worse than the reality and, as was often the case, James ended up wondering why it had been on his mind for so long.

Once the main presents were opened and the family sat down for lunch, Lewis's questions started. What was high school like? How come James was so tall? Was his voice breaking yet? Was Malika his girlfriend?

"I heard Mum talking to Auntie Sally on the phone, she mentioned a girl called Malika. Does she like you? I bet you like her, don't you?"

James went bright pink. Not in a million years would *anyone* think of him in that way. Lewis continued on his path towards ultimate awkwardness for James.

"I suppose it would be difficult though, you going out with someone. What with you never talking and all that. Why is it you don't talk again?"

Uncle Jeremy broke off from regaling Sally about being the month's top salesperson at the car supermarket and the flashy watch he had bought with the commission.

"Lewis, take a breath will you? Why do *you* talk so *much*?" Uncle Jeremy barked with a smile. "Give the lad a break! Some of the greatest people in history were quiet. Five billion people watched Neil Armstrong become the first man to walk on the moon and he hated being the centre of attention. Rosa Parks made a historic stand for civil rights in America, she wouldn't say boo to a goose. Bill Gates and Mark Zuckerberg are two of the richest people in the world, and you know what? They're quiet people – nowt wrong with being quiet!"

Uncle Jeremy shoved a forkful of turkey into his mouth and the whole table stared at him.

"What?" he said, his mouth full. There was a stunned hush at this previously unknown cultural knowledge Uncle Jeremy had revealed. It struck a chord with James who made a mental note to Google famous shy people when he got home. Jessie, grabbing handfuls of mashed potato in her little fists and laughing as it oozed through her fingers, broke the silence. Uncle Jeremy wasn't finished. Taking a sip from the pint of beer in front of him, he continued.

"You know what James, if you are stuck for something to say – ask a question! There's nothing people like more than talking about themselves. I should know. If you can at least ask a question, you're part of the conversation – bingo!"

James wasn't sure it was that easy, but he could see the point. As usual with Uncle Jeremy, he quickly turned the conversation to making himself the main subject.

"When I started out in the car business, I was working with these old blokes who knew everything there was to know. They had been there and done it many times over. I had no idea what to say to them, they intimidated me, so that's what I did – I asked questions. Any opportunity for them to talk about their latest sales and triumphs and we'd strike up a conversation in no time. What I'm trying to say is, don't try to think of something to *say*, think of a question to *ask*. That might lead to another question and there's your conversation!"

When it was time to leave, Uncle Jeremy punched James playfully on the arm.

"You'll be ok, big guy, you'll be fine. Trust your Uncle Jeremy."

Everyone kissed and hugged at the doorway, but Paul and Uncle Jeremy hung back in the hallway. Uncle Jeremy handed Paul something that looked like a small folded piece of paper. Paul patted him on the shoulder and they shook hands.

"No problem, Paul. I've had a few good months for commission and I'll always do anything I can to help. You know where we are," Uncle Jeremy said.

As James belted himself into the car, Paul got in and flashed Sally a look that seemed to communicate something between them. The strange feeling of tension that hung over the family recently seemed to lift, and they sang Christmas songs to Jessie on the way home.

Chapter 14

The country was in the middle of a January freeze and James was tapping his feet up and down as he perched on the bench at school. He still refused to use the dinner hall. He hated this hour of the day – the lack of structure and proper supervision made James edgy. The pear incident meant he was on guard for trouble – he considered going somewhere else at lunch, but the options were limited. The cool pupils all hung out around the other side of the building on the picnic benches, and it seemed to James like there was a constant contest to try to prove how popular they were. It wasn't for him.

As usual, some of the other boys were kicking a ball around the square of tarmac – someone had brought in a proper football, albeit a battered one. James watched Tom and his talent stood out a mile, but he didn't feel so pleased for him anymore. James couldn't help the resentment bubbling away within him. Why couldn't Tom be talented *and* kind? It was possible to be both, surely? Every time Tom got the ball he left a trail of boys behind him as he dribbled around them and slotted the ball past Malika who was playing in goal. Malika was a handy goalkeeper and played for a local Hartlewich youth team. On the other side of the playground, a group of Malika's friends clapped and cheered. Tom turned away and ran past them kissing a pretend badge on his shirt and the girls giggled. Standing with his hands on his hips, Josh looked sullen.

The next time Tom received the ball, he added in a football commentary as he took the ball past his friends.

"And it's Tom Bailey in possession. He's dribbled it around one defender. He takes it on, sidestepping one way then the next. This boy's skills are truly something else. No one can get near him today. He's one to watch for the future that's for sure."

As Tom showboated with the ball, Josh snapped into action and suddenly charged in from the side, going in on Tom crudely with his foot raised, catching him heavily on the side of his knee. Tom's leg buckled sideways at a horrible angle. Screaming, he stumbled and dropped to the ground. Tom lay motionless, groaning – one arm covered his face, the other clutched his knee. Josh tried to take his hand and haul him up as the boys gathered round. Tom shrieked and wrenched his hand away. Whenever James's dad was watching football on TV and a player took a dive, he always said they couldn't be *that* injured if they were writhing around – it's when they don't move you worry. Well, Tom wasn't moving. James wanted to get up and check if Tom was ok but he couldn't, not with the other boys all there. Luckily, Malika had gone straight over and taken charge. She was crouching over Tom reassuring him and she had already dispatched some of the boys to get help.

Mr Ramos emerged from the school building with Mr Fellows looking concerned. They both bent down over Tom for some time, talking in low voices. The boys and Malika stood around them in a circle. Eventually, Mr Ramos helped Tom into a sitting position where he stayed for a minute or two, sucking in air between his teeth, tear stains down his face. Mr Ramos and Mr Fellows then counted to three and both lifted Tom, who shrieked again. He put his arms around their shoulders and they carried him into the building. James placed his sandwich back in his lunchbox – his appetite had gone.

Tom didn't return to school for the rest of the week. When James visited Mrs Samuel that Saturday, she was having what Cliff called 'a quiet day' with the TV on. Conversation was hard going. In the absence of anything else to do, James decided to text Tom:

Hey, you ok?

Tom didn't always respond to James's texts, but the three little dots popped up immediately which meant he was replying.

Not really. Lying in bed. I tore a knee ligament. Felt it rip and everything. It's going to take months, maybe even a year to heal, and that's only if I get specialist help.

James shuddered at the thought of anything 'ripping' and didn't really know what to reply. He wasn't sure what a knee ligament was but it didn't sound good to have torn one. He was never very good in situations where he needed to say the right thing to try and make someone feel better. He often came across as blunt or uncaring, but he just wasn't confident enough to know how to express sympathy. He'd blurt out something rubbishy and kick himself for it afterwards. Whatever had happened between them, he *did* feel sorry for Tom. Tom was a talented footballer on the cusp of following his dream and getting signed by a club – it must have been tough.

James couldn't think what to say that struck the right balance of understanding and positivity. At least when he communicated through text he had the time to think through a response. What he wanted to say was, *I don't like those boys, especially Josh, and I wish you didn't hang around with them*. Eventually, he played it safe and typed out a simple…

That's so rubbish, hope it gets better soon.

When Tom returned to school he was moving around awkwardly on crutches, a thick bandage wrapped around his knee. This was a bit of a novelty at first and his classmates swarmed around him firing questions at him. Some of Tom's friends were tasked with helping him around school – holding his bag when he moved between classes. At lunchtime, Tom was slumped on James's bench watching the others kick a ball around, his jaw clenched. He didn't say a word to James, who self-consciously nibbled his packed lunch, feeling like every eating noise was amplified by Tom's silence. Apologising for the incident, Josh seemed remorseful for about the first hour of Tom being back in school. He soon returned to his usual cocky self.

At first, the boys took their job of looking after Tom incredibly seriously, enjoying the responsibility and celebrity that came with being Tom's helpers. They also enjoyed the excuse to arrive at lessons late, ushering Tom in and pulling out a chair for him with great drama. The excitement of having a patient rely on them soon began to wear off. When James was moving between buildings for an afternoon lesson one day, he saw Tom and the boys ahead. James didn't like having people in front of him. Being a speedy walker, he had to concentrate on slowing himself down so that the boys stayed the same distance away from him. When they reached the building, they held the heavy door for Tom, waiting for him to come through.

"Come on Hobbles, we're not going to stand here forever. We've got lessons to get to, you know. We wouldn't want to be late!" Josh called to laughs. As Tom approached the door on his crutches, swinging and pushing gingerly with his good leg, the boys stepped backwards and let the door swing to a close with a thud. They made faces at the glass and walked off in hysterics. Tom tried to shoulder barge the door open, but the rucksack on his back slipped down his arm sending him off-balance. He wobbled backwards a few paces then toppled to the ground, landing on his bottom. His crutches clattered to the floor either side of him. Tom grimaced, the books from his rucksack scattered around him. A group of girls stepped past him as he struggled to get himself into a seated position. The same girls had been swooning over him only a week previously. Tom finally managed to shuffle himself into a position where he was sitting with his back to the wall.

"Here," said James, catching up. He crouched down and picked up Tom's books and tried to hand them to him.

"Put them in my bag, will you? I'm not going to sit here reading them, am I?" said Tom, gesturing to the rucksack on the floor. "I'm sick of this, sick of it. I just want to get off these stupid things and be able to walk properly and play football."

Tom kicked out at one of his crutches with his good leg. James picked up both crutches and offered a hand to Tom. Tom glared at it for a moment then took it, and James hauled him up. He waited as Tom hopped a few times to steady himself, then handed him his crutches. Tom got himself comfortable and James held the door for him. Tom stepped past him still glowering and they made their way to the next lesson.

James remembered Uncle Jeremy's advice about asking a question when he was stumped for something to say.

"Do…do you know any more about what is wrong with your knee?" James asked.

"Of course I do, it's had it. Busted. The ligament is completely ripped to shreds," Tom replied through his teeth.

James was quiet for a moment, he'd probably picked completely the wrong question to ask but he persevered.

"Can you get it fixed? Can they mend it?"

Tom snorted, "Well I need an operation, then months of physio. I'm on a massive waiting list for the operation, so can't have the physio until then. I'm probably making it worse all the time I don't have the operation, especially when people slam doors in my face. My dad looked into having an operation with a sports injury specialist to move things along a bit, but it was too expensive. I'm stuck like this on these stupid crutches. I'm literally never going to play football again."

"Oh," replied James, "that's... that's a shame."

James wasn't convinced about Uncle Jeremy's advice. He just seemed to be making Tom angrier, so he stopped asking questions. When they finally arrived at the lesson they were late. James hated arriving anywhere late. He was on time for *everything*. His dad called him a 'time lord' such was his obsession with making sure they arrived early for things. James held the door open for Tom, who headed straight towards the boys on the opposite side of the room.

"Got here did you? Where have you been?" asked Josh, pulling the knot on Tom's tie when he sat down.

James sat on the other side of the room, on his own. Waiting for Tom to sit down, the teacher turned to James with a frown. "James, you really need to try and get Tom here sooner, we've started the lesson."

There was a snigger from Josh on the other side of the room.

Chapter 15

The wintry gusts of wind cut through the boys' PE kits, causing them to shiver and wrap their arms around themselves. The school fields were exposed to the elements and the class were rubbing their hands together and blowing into them, some hopped from foot to foot. All James could think about was how good it was going to feel when they got back inside – he didn't even care it was art next. The art room would be warm, he'd have his uniform back on and PE would be over until the following week. Moments before they had come outside there had been an almighty downpour of hail, which sounded like gravel being thrown against the windows. Even staying in the awful changing room seemed preferable to this.

Mr Ramos ambled over from the school building. He was carrying a different mug in his hand, this one said 'P.E Teachers – like a normal teacher but way cooler'. He took a sip of coffee, then shouted and signalled to the boys to gather round. Tom was with him wearing a hoodie, thick coat, gloves and a hat. Children who weren't able to do PE usually had to go to another class, but Tom's parents had demanded he still be included in lessons even if he couldn't take part.

"Right lads, settle down and listen; cross country today and what a beautiful day for it!" Mr Ramos pulled his thick hood up over his head and grinned. "Luckily you don't need to worry about me; I've got myself wrapped up warm. Let's get your muscles moving and your blood pumping, and see how fit you all are. Today is just about seeing what you can do. We'll examine running techniques and strategy over the coming weeks. You're going to complete a simple course around the fields – across the football and rugby fields, over the all-weather hockey pitch, through the small wooded area, round the back of the wildlife area, through the long jump sandpit and down the running track for a triumphant finish. That's if you make it."

The boys made their way to the start line. Some started limbering up; doing what they imagined were impressive warm ups – crouching down and springing up, and stretching out their leg muscles. James was at the back of the group taking in the beautiful view beyond the fields to the distant hills, for a moment he was lost in it. There was a bird of prey floating on the bitter wind, ready to dive down and pounce on some unsuspecting creature it had in its sight.

"Listen, Jamie. You've got this." There was a voice behind him and James tensed, unsure who it was until he realised it was Mr Ramos. James's mind went into the usual frenzy of whirring sirens and flashing red lights at the suddenness of a social situation.

"Wh-what? I mean pardon, Sir?"

"This is what's going to happen, Jamie. *They* are all going to sprint off the moment we say 'go', desperate to be the one in front. Within five-hundred metres they'll be a sweaty panting mess; by a thousand metres they'll be just about managing to jog. By the time they finish they'll be walking to the finish line with their hands on their hips, with one almighty stitch. It's a marathon, kind of, not a sprint. Unless I'm mistaken, and I rarely am, you're going to make a decent runner Jamie. Take it steady and you'll be right up there at the finish. Save some energy and you might even be able to sprint the last hundred metres."

James stared at Mr Ramos, "Th…thank you, Sir."

Mr Ramos was already marching towards the boys, whistling shrilly with his thumb and index finger. "Right lads, in a line. Spread out! No cheating on this course, no cutting corners or I'll disqualify you. Tom, here, is going to set you off. Ready?"

Tom wedged his crutches under his arms and raised one arm: "Ready, steady… GO!"

James wasn't even on the starting line and watched the boys sprint off, just as Mr Ramos had predicted. James stumbled into a jog, aware there was a large distance between him and the rest of the group already. Some of the boys were already at the half-way line of the football field and heading towards the rugby pitch. James increased his speed and found a steady pace. He could feel the mud kicking up the back of his legs and his flimsy trainers weren't the most suitable for muddy ground – he didn't *do* sports gear. James crossed the rugby pitch, gaining ground – the boys at the back were already struggling to sustain their speed. James thought about increasing his pace but he was in a steady rhythm he felt comfortable with. He remembered what Mr Ramos had said – keep some energy in the locker for the finish. Crossing the AstroTurf, James overtook the first couple of stragglers at the back and this spurred him on. He continued to pass some of the other boys as he made his way into the wooded area at the end of the field. He had to slow down here – the path was muddy and the grip on his trainers wasn't up to it. If he went too fast he would slip and fall. Emerging from the trees, James tried to find a rhythm again. Some boys were running a few metres then stopping to walk, then trying again. Passing them with ease, there was just a small group ahead of him now. Leading the pack was Josh and a couple of his mates – they were still going at a good pace. These were the boys who played in all the school teams. They were athletic and used to competing.

James picked up his speed to a point where he felt just about comfortable. Feeling his body starting to protest, the burn of lactic acid began to rise up his calves. He skirted the wildlife area and back onto the sports field. Josh's two companions were dropping off and James overtook them. He sensed their panic as they saw someone pass, then realising *who* it was passing them, they tried to increase their speed again. James could tell they didn't have any life left in their legs. Approaching the long jump pit, Josh was in his grasp. Glancing back, he must have heard the sound of James's feet behind him.

"Eh? What the…?" he panted. His body jolted as he attempted to accelerate. James and Josh were neck and neck through the sand. It was heavy going on their legs and Josh barged him as they passed through, shoulder to shoulder. James nearly fell and Josh took the lead again. As they emerged from the sandpit, it occurred to James that all those months of walking the streets of his village had made him fit. Very fit. Josh's legs had turned to jelly and his feet struggled to adjust from sand to firm ground again. Increasing his speed to a final sprint, James joined the running track and the final 100m straight. At the finish, Tom was waiting, his mouth wide open. Mr Ramos was standing, arms folded, with a huge grin and a knowing nod. He looked at his watch as James thundered across the finish line and brought himself to a stop. Crouching down, James watched Josh lumber over the finish line and collapse to the ground.

"That's a pretty good time, Jamie. Good lad," said Mr Ramos with a smile. "One of the best I've seen for someone your age, and we've not even begun to get you trained up yet. That's decided, you'll be joining our athletics squad in the summer term."

Swinging over, Tom clapped James on the back. "That was pretty impressive, to be fair."

Straining to get his head off the ground, Josh glared at Tom and James, then dropped it back to the grass and covered his face with his forearm.

"COME ON SLOW COACHES, JAMIE HERE FINISHED TEN MINUTES AGO," Mr Ramos shouted across the field to the rest of the runners, who were now walkers.

Chapter 16

James was munching on some toast at the kitchen table. Winter was merging into spring and the sun streamed through the patio doors. It had been an ok week in school. No major social interactions that required hours of analysis or cringing over, and his recent PE lessons with Mr Ramos had done him a world of good. Sitting in the high chair at the other end of the table, Jessie had been eating some porridge from a little plastic bowl. For the last five minutes it had been far more interesting to spread it around the high chair table with her spoon.

"Jessie," James said in a gentle but firm tone, "Mummy will be cross. You need to eat your porridge. Here, I'll help you." He pushed his own plate forward and stood up. Sally walked into the room and put her phone face down on the kitchen surface. She washed up the few bits in the sink, glancing behind her at James feeding Jessie. She waited until Jessie had eaten enough.

"James," she said softly, "those blogs you do, well you know how we're really pleased that you are interested in them again, and it's such a nice thing to do for the village? Well…"

James sensed this wasn't going to be good.

"…I think you need to be careful about mentioning people's lives directly. It might not, well, they might not always be happy to be mentioned on the website."

"What do you mean?" James felt ambushed again. "I talk about the history of the village, it's mostly from Mrs Samuel's books and the stories she tells me. It's nice for her to know she's still part of the Historical Society. She said it helps keep her going. *She* told me to write the blogs."

"I know, love. You've done a great job. But maybe just delete some of her more recent recollections, just the ones that are more about her and her family – maybe the ones mentioning John. You can't be too careful, that's all."

James was furious. The blogs had taken ages. He wrote about the stories Mrs Samuel had told him because they had historic meaning; men wanting their sons to follow in their footsteps into industry and issues like that. His parents wanted him to do more with the website and when he did they wanted him to stop. It made no sense.

"I tell you what, I'll just take the whole stupid website down. I don't understand you, or Dad. You just want me to be a quiet loser forever because every time I do try to do something you just tell me off!"

"James…"

James was unable to listen to any more and he was shouting, his fury volcanic. "You never support me. It's no wonder I am like I am!"

The office door swung open and Paul's feet padded down the hallway.

"Dada!" Jessie chirruped and thrust her spoon in the air, sending a dollop of porridge onto her bib with a splat. Paul half-smiled at Jessie then turned to James.

"What's going on now? They'll hear you down the street."

"I want to live somewhere else. Somewhere on my own. Just me." James spat. He knew he was being childish, but the thought of living on an island by himself appealed to him. Hiding himself away from the world without the stress of having to think what to say to people would solve most of his problems as far as he could see.

"James, don't be so ridiculous. All we do is try and help you. Fine, go and live somewhere else and see how you get on. You know what? You could try thinking about others for a change – not just yourself," Paul snapped. It felt strangely satisfying to release some of his own frustrations and he couldn't stop himself.

"Paul…" said Sally with exasperation, trying to interject.

"Jay, Jay! Dada!" Jessie chirruped.

"No, Sally. I've had enough of him stropping around the house and taking his teenage angst out on us. It's not acceptable. Our whole lives revolve around him and his, well, his…"

James glared at Paul, willing him to finish the sentence. His *what*?

"You know what? I need to get some fresh air – clear my head," Paul said.

Jessie chose that moment to launch her bowl into the air. It crashed to the floor and sent a splattering of porridge across the kitchen tiles. Everyone stared at the mess. Jessie giggled nervously, waiting for the reaction.

"For goodness' sake," Paul muttered, ripping his jacket off the back of a kitchen chair and stomping back in the direction of the front door. He wrenched it open and just had time to hear James mutter that he wasn't even a teenager yet, before shutting it behind him with a slam. Standing on the step for a moment, he bowed his head before sauntering off.

Paul didn't really know where he was going. He marched through the streets of Hartlewich with his hands thrust in pockets, eyes to the ground. Eventually, the rhythm of his walking began to calm him and he started to take in his surroundings. These were the streets where he grew up, the roads where he played as a boy. Everywhere he walked, each corner he turned, there was a childhood memory – the little square of grass where he played football; the street where he played Kerby; the friend's front garden where they climbed trees; and the large bushes where he found a dead mouse. Replaying each of the memories, he realised he was always slightly separate from the group, always hanging back, on the outside of the action. The quiet one.

Passing the village green and the little row of shops, Paul was heading out of the village. His legs took him left, into the empty Village Hall carpark with the church ahead. Paul made his way through the lychgate and up the sweeping path to the gabled porch of the church. He

turned the heavy metal doorknob and was about to give the wooden door a push, but heard voices from inside the church and changed his mind. He went and sat down on the bench by the church building, taking a few deep breaths. The adrenaline pumping through him had eased and he felt exhausted – not so much by the walk, but by life in general. Things hadn't been easy recently. Maybe he should do this more often, he thought. Get out into the fresh air and the sunshine, stop cooping himself in that tiny office worrying about where the next contract was coming from.

Reflecting on his recent conversations with James, Paul groaned, putting his head in his hands – he wondered how he was getting everything so wrong. A clang from the porch door made him sit up again. Reverend Varga and another lady had appeared, smiling. They kissed cheeks and the lady made her way off down the path. Paul knew Reverend Varga from around the village and always said hello, but he had never spoken to her properly. He waved casually then went to pull out his phone, but thought better of it. He was beginning to dread looking at his phone – there was no escape from the work emails demanding his time, and notifications from his banking app telling him what he already knew: he needed more money in his account.

Reverend Varga closed the church door and was rummaging through a huge set of keys. Locking the door and pushing it to double-check, she started walking over to where Paul was sitting. Paul sat up awkwardly, crossed and uncrossed his feet, and whistled.

"You enjoying the peace of our wondrous churchyard?" Reverend Varga asked, sweeping her hand through the air at the landscape before her.

"Ha, yes, well, I need a bit of peace right now," Paul replied, playing with his wedding ring.

"Life is bringing you some stress at the moment? It happens to every one of us at times," she replied, sitting next to him.

"I suppose so." Paul suddenly felt the need to get things off his chest. He always had the habit of keeping things to himself, trying to protect others from his problems. He wanted to provide for his family, look after them and keep them safe, not bother them with *his* issues. He felt he could offload on Reverend Varga and she would listen without judgement, so that's what he did. He told her how he'd had a good relationship with his son, but it had derailed recently and he didn't know how, or why. Things were different between them and he felt sure *he* was probably the cause of it. It felt good to tell someone, but even better to finally say out loud that their money situation was causing him sleepless nights. He was biting his nails, something which he hadn't done since he was a child, and losing weight. When he left his job to set up his own IT business, it had gone well and maybe he'd got complacent. Income began to plateau and customers drifted off to bigger, more established companies who could offer more than just a personal touch.

Reverend Varga listened, and ummed and ahhed in suitable places. When Paul had finished, she was silent and he regretted opening up. Maybe he had misread the situation. Maybe Reverend Varga was simply being polite, and she'd had to sit and listen to him witter on for ten minutes when she had better things to be doing. He felt embarrassed. But eventually she spoke.

"You know, my children are teenagers, a little bit older than the age of your son and it is not easy. When children start to grow up, you need new ways of parenting, new ways of communication and it can be like a daily battle trying the get that right. Lord knows, I made lots of mistakes, as we all will. What you are ultimately doing is learning to let children go. They are older, wanting their independence, but also still requiring of your guidance and reassurance. It feels like you are losing your control because they suddenly have more of a voice. When you first have a baby it is totally dependent on you. You have *full* control. But from that day there is a constant renegotiation of that dependence. The child takes more and more of the power from you. You can show you are interested in the little things they talk about, even if you haven't the faintest clue *what* they are talking about. Then they will be happier discussing the big things with you if they need to. You have big worries about your business which might mean you have overlooked the little things, maybe? These are my thoughts."

Paul nodded. She was right. James had faced a big challenge in his life and he'd been so bogged down in his own issues that he had ignored James's problems, or worse, he'd found them irritating. He'd had his own worries and couldn't deal with James's too. James had always struggled – like the time he first went to swimming lessons when he was younger and he had to sit on the side of the pool for about the first five lessons, wrapping his arms around himself and sobbing. He kept turning round to see where Paul was and in the end the swimming teacher suggested Paul left so he was out of sight, and eventually James got in. But why did he have more patience then? Paul wondered.

"The worst thing is," said Paul, shaking his head, "I was like him when I was young. I was shy. I was awkward. I struggled to speak to people. In fact, I still do. If Sally, my wife, suggests we go out with friends at the weekend, I spend all week worrying about it. It's hard for her to understand being the wonderfully gregarious extrovert that she is. How could anyone not enjoy going out? How could anyone not like the chance to socialise and chat? We've always said that she is the glitter and I am the glue, but I feel like I'm coming unstuck. I find those things difficult so it's no surprise that James does too. I want to tell him he will be ok, he'll find himself. I used to do that. I used to reassure him, but I've stopped."

"Then that's what you should do. But children expect us to be a little bit annoying, it's all part of the parenting game." Reverend Varga chuckled and stood up. "Your son sounds like a most caring and considerate young man who is sensitive to others. He might challenge you from time to time but you know you are immensely proud of him. Maybe at the first opportunity you tell him?"

He would, Paul thought, he definitely would. He *had* to try harder.

Chapter 17

The laptop was switched on but James's focus wasn't. He was sitting on the settee trying to do homework. Sally was grabbing a quick shower, so James was assigned the job of watching over Jessie. She was racing from one settee to another, giggling as she crashed into the cushions – she could entertain herself for hours doing this. Every now and then James would offer her a fist bump. She loved this and would need at least five fist bumps before she would carry on with her game.

On the arm of the settee next to James, Sally's phone buzzed and a message appeared.

"Mum, message!" he called over his shoulder. He heard the shower running from the bathroom upstairs. James tilted her phone towards him in case it was from Dad, or something else important.

Thanks.

It was from 'John'. James stared at it – it seemed so impersonal. The texts James had seen Sally send or receive

100

always ended in an 'x' or a smiling emoji. This message felt cold. How many 'Johns' did his mum know? He'd only ever had a conversation about one John with her. John Samuel. James hesitated, searching his conscience. He knew his mum's security code, he'd seen her enter it so many times. Quickly tapping it in, James knew full well what he was doing was wrong and he was betraying Sally's privacy but he couldn't stop himself. The flowing water stopped and the shower door slid open upstairs. Sally's apps were all in a different layout to the ones on his phone so it took a few swipes to find her messenger app. It seemed to take an age to open, their wi-fi wasn't the quickest and Paul always complained that it drove him up the wall when he was trying to work. Sally was humming upstairs and Jessie was now feeding a doll with a toy bottle. She didn't have the gentlest parenting skills and dropped the doll on its head. Finally, the app opened and James was met with a chain of messages from John Samuel. Skimming through, each one made James's blood boil. John had messaged Sally to demand that 'her son' remove all the blog posts on the website that included any mention of his parents' lives and especially any references to him. It was private family business, he said. He questioned why James needed to go to the care home every Saturday and was it really an appropriate place for a young boy? James, he said, was confusing his mum by raking up the past all the time.

For every message John Samuel had sent, Sally had calmly supported James, wondering how many twelve year olds would give up their Saturday afternoon to go and see an old lady in a care home. She said his blogs were written purely for historical reasons and James wouldn't have thought for one minute they would have caused upset. John's responses were cutting – a *normal* twelve year old wouldn't be hanging around a care home and it would suit James far better to play with mates his own age. There was a gap of a few days, a period James guessed when Sally was quietly seething to herself. Then she messaged to tell John that James probably wasn't a 'normal' twelve year old, whatever 'normal' was, and that was why he was so special, but he had now deleted the blogs as requested.

Hearing the landing creak and footsteps on the stairs, James double-clicked and swiped out of the app. He put the phone back on the arm of the settee and pretended to be deep in thought with his homework. Sally wandered into the room, rubbing her hair on a towel. Jessie was in a phase where everything Sally did, she had to experience too.

"Mama, tow. Mama, tow!"

"Jessie wants her hair drying with the towel too?" Sally asked, reaching down and giving Jessie's hair a pretend ruffle with the towel. Sally left the towel draped on Jessie's head and her muffled giggles could be heard as she tried to pull it off.

"Right, thanks James. You can get off now. Thanks for watching over Jessie. You wouldn't believe how hard it is to grab a shower round here."

James shut down the laptop and snapped it closed. To Sally's surprise he jumped up and gave her a tight hug.

"See you later. Love you. Thank you, Mum."

Cliff was mopping the floor in the entrance hall at Grange Manor.

"Ahh, hello Mr James." Then, reading James's expectant eyes, "Today is a quiet day for Mrs Samuel, James."

James nodded, disappointed. On quiet days, he grieved for the Mrs Samuel who chatted away about the past. As he walked past Mr Adamson's room, James noticed that he had a shiny briefcase by his chair. It was made from dark brown leather and matched his smart shoes. James stopped.

"Oh, are...are those your papers to sign, Mr Adamson?"

Mr Adamson smiled and tapped the side of his nose.

"Cliff had my briefcase sent over from the office, lad. Got some important papers here, could be a big case. That's why clients choose Adamson's Solicitors – best in the business. I'm just going through the legalities. Can't say too much right now."

Mrs Samuel was sitting on her chair. Her eyes flickered in James's direction when he walked in but she didn't acknowledge him.

James poured her some water out of the jug and sat down on the bed beside her. She sat forward.

"Which way is west?" she asked.

"I... err...pardon?"

"West, which way is west? I think I need to head west to get home." She tried to turn her head towards the window to look outside.

"I...I don't know, I'm really sorry," James said

awkwardly. He got up to look at Mrs Samuel's visitors' book. He was surprised to notice John Samuel's name.

"Your son has been to visit. John. He's visited?" He realised he said it more as an accusation than a question and changed his tone. "Was it, erm, nice to see John?"

"John?" Mrs Samuel looked confused, and she sat back deep in thought. "Now you mention it, a man was talking about a house. Was that my house? Was that John? I didn't understand half of it. All sounded very technical and businesslike. I just need Harry to visit now, he's always late. He'll know what to do. He's probably having a few ales down the Working Men's Club after work."

James didn't know what to say, so busied himself writing his name in the book. Mrs Samuel relayed the story she had told him many times about how Harry had once forgotten it was John's birthday party and had gone crown green bowling instead and John had thrown his bowl of jelly at the wall in anger. James didn't think *that* story would be going on the blog anytime soon!

"I want to ask Harry something, I mustn't forget. There was a song he used to sing when John was little. Can't for the life of me remember what it was. His flowers too, I need to ask about his roses."

James finished writing in Mrs Samuel's book and sat down on the bed.

"What about them, Mrs Samuel? The roses I mean."

"Well, Harry always grows me my rose each year, Julia's Rose. It's not easy to grow, mind. It's copper orange and smells beautiful. I'm not sure anyone else could grow them like Harry."

James smiled to himself. Last year he had toiled in his garden for months growing a Julia's Rose bush so she had a bunch for Harry's grave.

Mrs Samuel gazed at the pictures on the wall for a while until her eyes looked heavy and she started to doze. Cliff came to the doorway.

"Ok, James? A penny for them?" James looked confused. "A penny for your thoughts? You look sad, James. Anything on your mind?"

James looked at the floor, then the wall. Eye contact wasn't his strength.

"I feel… I feel like I'm losing her a bit. Like we're all losing her. She feels, I don't know, kind of distant. Like the real Mrs Samuel is hiding inside and only comes out sometimes."

"I understand, James. She's in there alright. She will have good days and quiet days, we just have to do all we can to make sure she has as many good days as possible."

"But what can we do? I feel like the real her is slipping away." James felt tears welling in his eyes.

"It's simple, James. We carry on doing what we're doing – showing kindness and patience. We can also make sure she gets lots of reminders, things that will jog her memory – talking points, anything that will focus her and help her to chat. The best thing is to surround her with people and things that are important to her."

James nodded. As Mrs Samuel snoozed, he sat there feeling helpless, but it dawned on him there was one thing he *could* do.

Chapter 18

Jessie was in a niggly mood and screamed blue murder every time James tried to put her down. It was easier to carry on walking around the house with her in his arms. She was in one of those frames of mind where she was only seconds away from a full-blown tantrum. Like most two year olds, if Jessie had a tantrum, she could make them last for ages. Once the tantrum started, nothing would be right for Jessie. She'd scream because she wanted a story, scream that she didn't want a story, then scream because she hadn't had a story – it was lose-lose for anyone caught in the crossfire. Sometimes Sally and Paul would try to analyse why Jessie was having the tantrum – she was either overtired, or not tired enough, or hungry, or she'd eaten too much, or she was teething. James couldn't keep up and always tried to avoid the scene. Sally was on the phone to Grandma and Paul was working in the office, so he didn't have much choice this time.

Circling the kitchen, he bounced Jessie up and down in his arms willing Sally to hurry up. When Sally and

Grandma got talking, they could *talk*. James idly glanced down at the local newspaper which was folded on top of the kitchen table. The front page caught his attention immediately – there was a large picture of Hartlewich Church. James plonked Jessie down on the floor – she screeched and held her arms up to him.

"I'm sorry Jessie, I've got tired arms – you're getting heavy!" James passed her a set of toy keys which seemed to placate her and she jiggled them up and down. James unfolded the paper and read the headline.

Church Controversy: Gravestones to Go!

Why would anyone want gravestones to *go* anywhere? That was someone's memorial – about the only visible evidence they had lived and contributed to village life. He scanned the article, already feeling indignant.

Hartlewich residents have questioned the decision by the Parish Council to remove between twenty and thirty gravestones from the churchyard at the village church. Work is intended to take place during the summer, on apparent safety grounds. The gravestones affected are mainly of the monument style, with a heavy block base and a tall cross or pillar, but also some of the older upright headstones. They will either be dismantled and laid on the ground, or removed completely to an area around the back of the church. A Parish Council meeting will take place in June to finalise the safety measures. Residents have been invited to attend to give their views. Peter Birtwistle, whose family have owned the butchers in Hartlewich for over one hundred years, expressed his dismay:

"This is an act of vandalism. Some of those gravestones have been there for over 200 years. It's like erasing history. It's health and safety gone mad."

However, Humphrey Fossington-Smythe, long-standing Chairman of the Parish Council, was clear in his reasons for the action:

"We have a legal duty of care to ensure the churchyard is safe and that people can visit the church secure in the knowledge that no gravestone will topple over on them. The most financially sound option is to remove them in a sensitive and respectful manner. We feel sure that we will have the full support of the village residents when making these difficult decisions."

You don't have my full support, thought James. How dare they? Paul wandered in from the office with an empty mug and flicked on the kettle.

"Dada, Dada!" Jessie called, her arms stretching up to him. He reached down and picked her up with a dramatic groan and she bopped him on the head with the keys.

"You're getting big, Jessie. Too many biscuits!"

"Bisca, bisca!" Jessie cried, pointing at the biscuit tin.

"Schoolboy error mentioning biscuits," Paul muttered, smiling at James. "What's up?"

James was still staring at the newspaper. "This is terrible," he said.

"Oh, I know," Paul replied sagely. "That local paper is rubbish these days. There's nothing in it – written by a journalist in an office twenty miles away who's never even visited the area."

"I… I mean the headline. The story. This!" James jabbed the paper with his finger. "They're getting rid of gravestones. How can they get rid of gravestones?"

"Oh, I see." Paul took the newspaper from James and scanned it. "Well I guess it *is* a safety thing. They might fall on someone, I suppose."

James got that, he really did, but surely there was something else they could do rather than getting rid of them. Even laying them down on the ground meant the grass would grow over them.

"It's not fair. It's not fair on those people or their families. It's… it's… disrespectful!" James's anger was growing.

"Well, you've got two options, James. You either try to understand and accept it, or you fight it."

James looked him in the eye and Paul knew immediately which one of those two options his son was going to take.

Chapter 19

James pulled the hood of his grey jersey over his head, despite it being a mild spring day. He wore his usual faded grey jeans and tatty white trainers. When James found clothes he felt comfortable in, he stuck with them until they were so worn his mum had to beg him to try some new ones. He liked his mum to buy two of everything if possible because when he found something he liked, he wanted to make sure he could always wear it even when one set was in the wash. Grey was pretty much his colour of choice – it was neutral and wouldn't draw attention to him. Malika had once told him his look was 'geek chic' and he didn't really know how to take it, but she was smiling so he presumed it wasn't a bad thing. James saw the boys from school playing football on the village green. Tom was standing with his crutches on the sideline and was looking down at his phone. One of the boys shouted something and they all stopped and laughed in James's direction. Tom hopped round to have a look then turned back to the pitch.

It was no surprise where James was heading. He needed to investigate these appallingly dangerous gravestones for himself. Beyond the sandstone wall, the churchyard stretched out in front of him. He wondered how anyone would want to do *anything* to change this. The familiar path swept up to the left, a patchwork of ancient paving stones. James surveyed the grassy area where he had helped to locate Mrs Samuel's grandmother in the unmarked paupers' area and the neat rows of newer graves made of polished marble, giving way to the randomly placed older gravestones which were a grey-green colour and made of stone. He looked up at the beautiful church tower guarding them, and the sun shining through the building making the stained glass windows glow in an array of beautiful colours.

James examined some of the older gravestones which he presumed would be on the condemned list. They were mottled with moss and lichen and some had chips in the stonework, but they didn't look any different to how they had always looked. James knew the history of almost everyone in the older section of the churchyard, Mrs Samuel had made sure of that. What he didn't know was much about the actual gravestones themselves. James Googled 'old gravestone types' on his phone. He found a great website which told him all about the designs of the gravestones in the churchyard. The upright gravestones were usually either a gothic, or classical style. Some of them were carved with flowers or wheat, or even a skull and crossbones – each having some kind of meaning. There were chest tombs – a rectangular box shape made of stone with a thicker piece of flat stone on top. A couple of the graves had a square column with a large stone pot on top, to represent a funeral urn, or a large carved angel. There were many other types of gravestone that James identified in the graveyard that afternoon. They were a memorial to someone's life but these stone sculptures were also beautiful works of art, created by skilled stone masons. They needed preserving, not tearing down.

Are you ok?? Xx.

A text from Sally popped up on James's phone.

Hi, yes, I'm just at the church. There was something I needed to do xx

Yes, your dad said you might be. Come home soon, ok? Going to start tea in a min xx

On his way back, the boys were still playing football in the distance and Tom was standing in the same position. He had put a coat on. James tapped out a text:

How's the knee?

He saw Tom reach into his pocket and pull out his phone. He read the text then glanced around before replying.

I'm sick of it. It's really painful and I hate not being able to do anything.

Have you had a date for your operation?

Nope!

James texted back to say that he was sorry, but Tom didn't reply.

The next day was Sunday and James had jobs to do, which was good because it took his mind off the usual Sunday anxiety. The first was to get into the garden and sort his flower beds out. They needed some serious maintenance. His second job was to blog on his website about the beauty of the gravestones. There was also the small matter of the petition James wanted to set up with his dad's help for villagers to object to the Parish Council's plans.

"How will people know the petition is there?" James asked Paul, after it went live. "I only get about fifty hits to the website a month."

"I suppose you need to raise awareness. Make a 'Sign the Petition' poster and ask Peter Birtwistle if you can put it in his shop window. Maybe you could ask your school if you could put something in the newsletter?"

James thought about this for a moment. Anything that made him more visible at school was a definite no-no. But it *did* give him another idea.

Chapter 20

James stood in the doorway of Mrs Samuel's room with a brown envelope in his hand – it was tied in a pink ribbon. The bed was neatly made and the chair beneath the window empty.

"Not to worry James, we haven't asked her to leave, she's catching some rays with Mr Adamson." Cliff was making his way down the corridor. He both walked and talked in an equable manner which always put James at ease. James looked blank. "She's outside, James, on the patio with Mr Adamson. They're sitting in the sun. They've become quite the partners in crime round here, I can tell you. When they're together they're nothing but trouble. She's tired today, they had a yoga session this morning. You should have seen them all stretching in their chairs," Cliff smiled.

Mrs Samuel and Mr Adamson were side-by-side in their wheelchairs with their backs to James. They both had matching blankets tucked over their knees. Grange

Manor had a small and simple garden, with a square patio and a stretch of stripy grass with a bird bath in the middle. There were some flower beds and a high wooden fence.

"Hello," James said, coming round in front of them. They both looked up at him and Mrs Samuel shielded her eyes from the spring sunshine. Mr Adamson lifted his pork pie hat in acknowledgement.

"Pull up one of the chairs, James," Laura called through the patio doors from the residents' lounge.

James dragged one of the chairs over and perched on the edge of it.

"There's roses over there, son," Mrs Samuel said. "My Harry loves his roses."

"Yes," said James, looking over at the flower beds, "so do I. It… it was because of you, and Harry, I grew lots of roses like them."

"Oh I know, son. All those blooms at the churchyard," Mrs Samuel looked at Mr Adamson. "Beautiful it was, roses everywhere. Just beautiful."

James could have jumped up and hugged Mrs Samuel for remembering the Village Fair.

"You can't beat a freshly cut rose, Julia. I gave one to my true love every single Valentine's Day," said Mr Adamson.

Laura came out from the residents' lounge and straightened the blankets on Mrs Samuel's and Mr Adamson's knees.

"Cup of tea, you two?" she said.

"Yes please, dear. The usual – splash of milk and one sugar. Julia, tea?" said Mr Adamson, taking charge. He didn't wait for a reply. "That's two teas, one with a splash of milk and one sugar. One well-brewed, a bit more milk, but no sugar. Thank you," said Mr Adamson curtly.

Laura looked at James and rolled her eyes affectionately.

"You want one, James?" she asked.

"Oh…no, but thank you," he replied.

While they waited for the tea, James took his chance. "Mr Adamson, I've… I've got another case for you. A real one this ti…I mean, an important case. I need your help."

Mr Adamson peered at the envelope and the pink ribbon, narrowing his eyes.

"We're not taking on any more cases at the moment, lad. We're overrun in the office. We're not the most in-demand solicitors in the area for nothing." He glanced at the envelope again.

"If you had ten minutes sometime, would you have a look? If you're not too busy, I mean. They're getting rid of lots of the older gravestones up at the church and… and I don't want them to. The Parish Council – I don't want them to do it. In the envelope is the guidance that churches have to follow and I… I was wondering if there were any loopholes which would stop them. It's a big document."

Mr Adamson's eyes twitched, but he remained resolutely composed.

"I tell you what I'll do, we've got bigger cases going on than this, much bigger, but if I get a spare moment I'll cast my eye over it. I make no promises though, lad."

"Thank you," James said, leaning forward and handing over the envelope. Mr Adamson quickly tucked it down the side of the wheelchair and patted it to signify it was in safe hands.

"You'll stop them, son. Don't you worry," Mrs Samuel said. "Talking of the churchyard, I want to see Harry's grave, son. I keep asking them if I can go." She thumbed behind her in the direction of the building.

Laura reappeared with the tea.

"Here we go," said Mr Adamson. "Come on, drink up Julia. Let's get this tea down us, I've got work to do. I can't sit here doing nothing *all* afternoon."

Chapter 21

As April turned to May, James was spending more of his spare time out in the garden, tending to his rose bushes, nurturing them into life again. He was more relaxed about it this year with no major reason for them to grow other than to make the garden look nice. There was one rose bush he was particularly keen to look after. The copper-orange Julia's Rose was notoriously hard to grow, but he was determined to do it again this year. He was also researching a speech for Paul to read at the Parish Council meeting the following month. James felt fired up and cross about what was happening, but he'd *never* stand up in front of people himself. What he really needed though was some legal expertise; he would have to wait for Mr Adamson's opinion on the matter before he could make a proper start.

James still missed primary school and he thought about it all the time. It had taken a while, but he'd settled into more of a routine in Year 7. One day he was sitting eating his sandwiches when he sensed a figure approaching from the left. Tensing, he turned to see Mr Ramos standing next to his bench, watching the footballers and humming under his breath. Eventually he spoke.

"It's summer term now, Jamie. Athletics season is here. We've got club night starting next Tuesday, 3.30 to 4.45. I'm pretty certain we can turn you into a half-decent 800m or 1500m runner, cross country is a given too. You'll be coming, won't you?" Mr Ramos didn't look at James, instead he continued watching the boys from James's year boot the battered ball around. Mr Ramos put his thumb up at Tom who was leaning against the fence opposite. James tried to come up with some kind of half-coherent answer that wouldn't have him covering his head in embarrassment all night.

"I think so. I would need to get fitter, I think. I walk a lot, but don't run much."

Mr Ramos sighed as Josh scored and ran to the side of the playground, shushing a pretend crowd with his finger to his lips as the other boys ran over, patting him on the back and putting him in a celebratory headlock. "You're fitter than that rabble over there, but we'll get you in shape don't worry. Next Tuesday – don't forget, Jamie."

Mr Ramos turned and began to walk away.

"Mr Ramos, my… my name is James. It's James."

On the way home that day, James took a detour.

"Is Mrs Shah here? Can I just see her for a minute? I… I know she might be busy." James was at the front desk at his old primary school talking to the receptionist.

"Oh, hello James! I think she's still in her classroom.

I'm sure she won't mind you calling in. Just fill in this visitor's badge and I'll take you down there."

As he followed the receptionist across the hall, the school had that strange feeling when there were no children and everywhere was quiet – like the soul was missing from the building. When he reached his old Year 6 classroom, he waited in the corridor. He heard the receptionist say something and Mrs Shah exclaim. The receptionist beckoned him in and exited. James saw Mrs Shah sitting at her desk marking a pile of books.

"James! How wonderful, come in!"

James stepped inside the doorway. Apart from the different displays on the walls, very little had changed, but it *felt* different – and smaller, it seemed smaller. It didn't feel like *his* classroom anymore, it felt like it belonged to other children now.

"I need help. Erm... again."

"I hope it's not more rose growing advice, I was pretty rubbish at that," Mrs Shah said smiling. "Ok, well let's hear it and I'll see what I can do."

"Well I... I was just wondering if you could mention my petition about the graveyard in your school newsletter. They want to take down lots of the old gravestones and... and I don't think they need to. There are other things they could do to protect them. Hardly anyone has signed the petition on my website."

Mrs Shah sat back in her chair.

"I'm sure we can do that, James. I'll have to check with Mrs Barton first, of course. I'll write a few lines and include a link to your website."

"Thank you, thank you very much," James replied, relieved.

"How is school now, James. Ok?"

James thought for a moment. The issue with the churchyard and his desire to get back into his garden had definitely made him feel more positive. Mr Ramos asking him to take part in his athletics club had given him a boost too.

"It's ok. I miss here. I still...still find it hard to..." James didn't really know where he was going with that sentence. He still found it hard to do lots of things. Mrs Shah saved him:

"I understand, James. You know, there's a Hindu saying, *You become that which you believe you can become.* Look what you achieved last year. Try to believe in yourself and what you're doing, and it'll come good."

James half-smiled. "I'm going to go now. Thank you for seeing me, and for the newsletter."

"Bye, James. Oh, and James? You're doing great things. The village is lucky to have you."

As he passed the village shops towards home, James spied Tom on his own, slouched on the bench outside the convenience store. His injury seemed to have levelled out the balance of power between the two and he shifted uncomfortably when he saw James.

"Hi Tom," said James, not really feeling there was much option but to say something. "Are... are you ok?"

Tom looked up. He momentarily thought how much James had grown.

"Yeah, I'm ok. I guess. I was going down to town with Josh and my mates but they didn't turn up. Think I just slow them down and cramp their style."

"Oh, I'm sorry," replied James.

"It's ok, I *do* cramp their style *and* slow them down. I can't go home because I told my mum and dad I was out and neither of them are home from work until after five."

"Oh, I'm sorry," James said, aware he was repeating himself every time Tom said something. He didn't know what else to say. He could invite Tom to his, but that could be awkward if his dad was trying to work or Jessie was having a tantrum.

"I think I'm going to go to the care home to see Mrs Samuel," James pointed up the main road. "If you're able to get up there on your crutches?"

James felt ridiculous. Why on earth would Tom want to come to see Mrs Samuel? What would they all talk about? What if Mrs Samuel is having a quiet day? He immediately regretted it.

"Might as well. Better than sitting here in the rain," he said to James's surprise. "I've got nothing better to do."

After being let in by Laura, James and Tom took the lift up to the first floor. Mr Adamson called out from his room.

"I've been working on your case, lad. I'm just looking into the finer details. I'll give them what for when I'm up there in front of them at that meeting. They won't know what's hit them when I'm in full flow."

"You're coming to the meeting?"

"Of course I am, lad! I'm your representative. That's

what you're paying me for," replied Mr Adamson, as if James had just asked a ridiculous question.

"Oh, well, that's great," replied James, glancing at Tom. "We're just here to see Mrs Samuel."

"Righto, I'll get back to this." He waved the document at James.

"You're paying *him*?" asked Tom as they neared Mrs Samuel's room.

"No, not exactly, but he is doing a proper job for me. I think. I mean, I haven't seen exactly *what* he's doing, but I'm sure it'll be useful."

Perching on Mrs Samuel's bed, James introduced Tom as he sat down gingerly, his crutches propped against the wall.

"I wish I could get you both a cup of tea and a biscuit," said Mrs Samuel. "I hate not being able to look after guests properly."

James was relieved – it seemed like a good day and Mrs Samuel chatted away. Looking a bit bored, Tom kept checking his phone, but he was polite enough when Mrs Samuel asked him a couple of questions about school.

"Hello, son," Mrs Samuel said suddenly, interrupting Tom telling her about how he'd been scouted for a local football team before his injury. For a horrible moment, James thought Mrs Samuel must have had one of her lapses in memory and was greeting them again as if they had just arrived. He followed her gaze and saw the figure of John Samuel filling the doorway, looking deeply unimpressed. He was wearing shiny brown shoes, navy trousers and a crisp white shirt. He had sunglasses tucked into a pocket on his chest and he held his car keys and his mobile phone in his hand.

"What's this, the local youth club?" he asked, glaring at Tom and James.

"Sorry, we'll go," said James, jumping up.

"No, no. Don't mind me. I've only come to see *my* mother. Why wouldn't I want two children sitting in her room when I arrive?"

James wondered for a moment whether he had ever heard John say anything that wasn't dripping in sarcasm. James felt he had no option but to sit back down again and there was a strained silence. John leaned against the chest of drawers looking at his phone. James struggled with a tense atmosphere so he started gabbling away to Mrs Samuel, giving her updates about the forthcoming Parish Council Meeting. He told her how he wanted to write a speech for his dad to read on his behalf, and how he was waiting to see what Mr Adamson came up with on the legal side.

"You're wasting your time there. If they're not safe, they're not safe. No matter what you say it won't change a thing. It's always the same in these situations." John Samuel cut James off mid-flow without even looking up.

"Well...I...there's...there's other options. I think," James replied, feeling crushed.

John shrugged. "When's the meeting?"

"It's... June 15th." James didn't want to tell John. He didn't want to give him any more information about it – he didn't deserve to know any more. He didn't care. He didn't seem to care about anything.

"I need to get going," said Tom, reaching for his crutches, "my mum's home now."

He struggled to a standing position.

"What's up with your leg?" John said, looking up from his phone just long enough to nod at Tom's heavily bandaged knee.

"Knee ligaments," said Tom, screwing up his face as he made his way to the door.

"Painful," said John. He said it without any feeling and his flippancy annoyed James – John had no idea of the impact it was having on Tom's life.

"Tom is a really good footballer. He's been scouted by a top team. He needs an operation but he's on a long waiting list," said James.

"That's bad luck," said John flatly, sitting down on Mrs Samuel's bed in the space left by Tom.

John's texts to Sally suddenly sprang into James's head – how he wasn't *normal* and how he spent his time hanging around a care home rather than with people his own age. James felt flustered, like he had something to prove.

"And my *other* friend, Malika, she's… she's a really good singer and desperately wants singing lessons, but she can't because her parents are so busy. She'll… she'll be professional one day!"

Tom and John both looked slightly startled by this outburst but said nothing.

"Who's Malika?" asked Mrs Samuel, looking confused.

No one replied, and Mrs Samuel continued to frown.

"John?" she said. "Can we go and see Harry's grave?"

John tutted and shook his head.

"I've told you, Mum, it's too much of a faff. We have to fill in a form to let you come out – maybe one day. I've got a lot on," he replied.

Mrs Samuel sighed and sat back, grinding her teeth together.

"Did you look through my vinyl records, John?" she said, a moment later. "I keep trying to remember that song. You know?"

"I don't know which one you mean, Mum. You and Dad were always playing music. I keep saying, I honestly don't know. I've shoved your records in our garage. All your stuff is taking up a lot of space since we sold your house."

James felt so sad. That stuff was eighty years of someone's life. He wanted to shake John Samuel. He had a lovely mum. She might not have always got everything right, but she was *his* mum. She took him for his first day at school, she dried his eyes when he was upset and put plasters on his knees when he got into scrapes. Saying a quick goodbye, James followed Tom who was already at the end of the corridor.

"Which way is west, John?" he heard Mrs Samuel say from behind him.

"What do you mean which way is west, Mum?"

"West. I think my home is west."

When James got home he checked his petition, hoping lots of signatures would have suddenly appeared.

"Why has hardly anyone responded? Why does no one care, Dad?" he asked Paul, who came and stood behind him and put his hands on his shoulders.

"Sometimes people only miss things when they are gone," Paul said. "People get wrapped up in their own lives – I think we can all be guilty of that sometimes."

There was only one new name on the list – Mrs Shah.

Chapter 22

As June approached, the rose beds in James's garden had transformed into a bloom of colour again. There weren't as many roses as last year but he still felt a satisfying sense of pride. Growing flowers was something he was a natural at, he hadn't even needed to refer to any books like last year, it all came back to him. James was also working on his contribution to the Parish Council meeting. Mr Adamson hadn't yet provided him with any advice – these things can't be rushed, he'd said. James had obsessed over any information he could find on the internet. There was lots of guidance provided to churches about burial grounds and their obligation to keep them safe – he hadn't understood much of it. Accepting why tough decisions needed to be made, James also had too much respect for the past villagers to let their memorials simply be taken away, but he couldn't help starting to doubt that Mr Adamson was going to come up with the goods.

In school, the first session of Mr Ramos's athletics club had arrived. James heard the whispers and sneers from Josh and his group, but then that was their intention.

"James has been asked to go to Athletics Club? That's hilarious! What *is* Mr Ramos thinking?"

Malika was there and not for the first time she stepped in and saved him as he stood alone, feeling exposed and awkward, waiting for Mr Ramos to arrive.

"James!" she exclaimed, bounding over to him. "You've come to the club! You and me are going to be in the Olympics together one day. Mr Ramos says I'm going to be good at anything to do with jumping because of my height. High jump, long jump, triple jump – you name it, I'm going to jump it!"

James couldn't help but let the boys get to him. However, there was a part of him that wanted to do well – to show them. Rather than walking around the village, he had begun to jog. The jogs soon felt too easy, so he increased his speed until he was running at pace on the streets each night. It made him feel good and he loved feeling fit. He was soon able to really push himself.

Aware it would look ridiculous, James knew he couldn't run in his usual attire of skinny jeans, grey t-shirt and hoodie. He needed some proper gear – or at least some joggers and a sportier looking t-shirt, but he felt ill at ease in anything other than his normal clothes. A few weeks previously they'd had a free dress day at school for a local wildlife charity whose mascot was a frog called Fred. The pupils were asked to 'Wear Red for Fred'. James dreaded free dress days. He hated not wearing his usual uniform and being forced to wear something different for 'fun'. He didn't like the change of routine, or the pressure of having to choose something to wear. Sally told him it wasn't compulsory and to just go in his uniform as usual, he could still donate to the charity. James felt this would make him stand out even more by not taking part. It was a no-win situation and he spent a week agonising over it. He hardly had any red clothes, and in the end he wore an old red t-shirt he'd found at the bottom of his drawer. In James's mind he still stood out like a sore thumb, even though *everybody* was wearing red.

Sally had taken James shopping for some running gear at the local town's sports shop. After twenty minutes of turning his nose up at every item of sports clothing she held up to show him, Sally eventually persuaded him to try some on by telling him that even though they were struggling for money, his dad still thought it was important James had some proper sports gear. James sighed, feeling guilty. Emerging from the changing room wearing some blue joggers, the newness felt weird to him.

"I can't wear these, look how baggy they are!" he said, pulling the joggers outwards. He knew he was sounding whiny and ungrateful.

"It's just because you're used to those skinny jeans, James. They're about two sizes too small so it's no wonder everything else feels baggy!"

In the end, James reluctantly chose some black training pants, which were quite slim and didn't feel too different from the fit of his jeans, a white t-shirt and a new pair of white trainers.

As the pupils stood waiting for Mr Ramos, Josh picked up one of the shot puts which were lying with all the equipment and started pushing it up and down in the air like he was weight lifting.

"Hey, lads, I bet James couldn't even pick this off the ground, never mind throw it." The boys guffawed in James's direction.

"That'll be the same James who had you all huffing, puffing and crying like babies when he left you standing at cross-country," replied Malika, giving them a look that said 'and don't bother replying'.

"Right everyone, gather round. Put that shot put down Josh, no one has asked you to touch the equipment. You never pick up anything without supervision. That's rule number one and not a great start for you," Mr Ramos called, ambling across the field towards them.

For the whole of the club session, James didn't say a word. He felt overwhelmed. He was out of his depth. But when he was asked to run, he *ran* and no one could get near him.

Chapter 23

I t was now only a few days until the Parish Council meeting and James was getting a bit panicky. On the way home from athletics, he jogged to the care home. When Laura let him in, a number of the residents were having tea in the lounge. Mrs Samuel was sitting at a table with a bowl of soup in front of her. One of the care workers was laughing as she tucked a tea towel into the neck of Mrs Samuel's jumper so she didn't spill the soup on herself.

"They've all had their hair done today, James. You should have seen Mrs Samuel with the hairdresser, she was as proud as punch. Mr Adamson had his beard trimmed – I think he terrified the hairdresser with his exacting instructions. I hope she comes back," said Laura, with a little laugh. "Mrs Samuel's just having a bite to eat, James. You're welcome to go in and sit with her."

"No it's ok. I'll just stick my head in and say hello. It's Mr Adamson I want to nip and see. Is that ok?"

"No problem, James," said Laura. "He's coming down for his tea in a while. He likes to book his time slot like he's eating somewhere fancy. I sometimes expect him to ask for a wine list. He's not shy in giving us his opinion on the food either!"

James opened the door to the resident's lounge and poked his head round.

"Mrs Samuel. Hi…" James called softly. Mrs Samuel continued to gingerly try the soup from her spoon. He tried again, a little louder.

"Mrs Samuel? Hello?" She still didn't acknowledge him and his confidence started to drain away as other residents began to look at him. The care worker, who was busy filling a kettle at the side of the room, turned and smiled at James. She went over to Mrs Samuel and put a hand on her forearm and pointed at James, who tried again.

"Hello, Mrs Samuel. I'm… I'm just saying a quick hello today but I'll come to visit you soon. I'm just bobbing up to see Mr Adamson."

Mrs Samuel looked at James, then the care worker. As James left he saw Mrs Samuel ask something and the care worker said his name to her.

Cliff was ahead of James as he climbed the stairs. "Ahh James, and how are you?" he asked, making his way in his usual steady manner. "You've got Mr Adamson fired up with this churchyard business. He's treating it like the court case of the century, making notes and practising his opening comments in the mirror. It's done him good."

When James arrived at Mr Adamson's room he was sitting in his chair, his trimmed beard making him look more like someone who used to be a solicitor.

"Just the person! Come in, come in. It's all done – I've got lots of notes for you. I've analysed all the relevant sections of the document and set out the case. In brief, I feel the Parish Council are being premature in their actions. Unless there is sufficient evidence to suggest the memorials are about to topple, they should be doing all they can to preserve them. Everything is here, Janice will invoice you forthwith." He handed over a weighty file, tied in a pink ribbon.

"Thank you, Mr Adamson. You're still coming to present the case?"

Mr Adamson's demeanour changed and he looked down, fidgeting with the gold cufflinks on his sleeve.

"Now, I've looked into that, lad. As much as I want to give them the what for, I don't think they will let me leave here, you see. It's like Fort Knox, there's no escape." He laughed nervously.

"Oh…well," James was slightly taken aback, "I'm sure I could have a word with Laura and Cliff and get something arranged. I think we just have to fill out a form. Cliff was just saying…"

"No, no lad. We don't want to cause a fuss and put people to trouble." He coughed. "As much as I want to be there, of course."

"I'm sure it won't be a prob…"

"The fact of the matter is, lad, on reflection and after a great deal of thought, I'm…well," Mr Adamson reached up and removed his hat from his head and placed it on his lap. "I'm, as I was saying, I'm… well, to be perfectly frank with you, lad… I'm… scared."

"You're… you're *scared*?" James noticed Mr Adamson's eyes fill with tears and he sat down, instinctively putting his hand on top of his. "Oh… that's… I mean… it's not a problem at all."

"You do it, lad. You do it," Mr Adamson whispered.

James smiled at him and held up the file.

"Don't worry Mr Adamson. We'll be fine now we've got your notes."

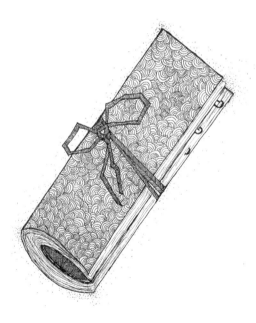

Chapter 24

When James got home he carefully untied the ribbon and opened the file. Mr Adamson had been forensic, highlighting points in the legal guidance James hadn't even noticed, never mind considered. Everything was written in fountain pen in beautiful cursive handwriting. Using this remarkable document, James stayed up late to finalise his speech for his dad to read at the meeting.

The day before the Monday meeting, James was restless, pacing the house. He didn't enjoy Sundays as it was, but he just couldn't settle. He went out into the garden and stood before his roses. Bees buzzed around them and a butterfly fluttered from bloom to bloom. James thought back to the previous year and remembered Beauty, the butterfly he'd rescued after finding it with a damaged wing. Half of the garden was in shadow, the trees at the back by the fence were blocking the light. The Julia's Rose bush was caught by a ray of sun, the rich copper colour sparkling in the bright light. Picking up the secateurs which were lying on the grass, James clipped off eight of the roses. He trimmed the thorns and arranged them into a bunch in his hands. One of the remaining roses on the bush caught his eye. It stood out from the others. The petals were perfectly formed, curling into a flawless spiral with a speckled, golden hue spreading up from the base. Holding it gently in his hand, James was mesmerised by the vibrant beauty of it. He clipped it off and added it to his bunch. He took the flowers inside and tied them with a piece of orange ribbon from the kitchen drawer.

"Jay, Jay. Flow, flows!" Jessie called, toddling in and pointing at the roses in delight. Paul followed.

"Hey, James… oh they're beautiful," he said, noticing the roses. "I think they're even better than last year if that's possible. Gosh, the rose in the middle is really something special."

"I think the soil was more nourished," James replied. "The more you work at it and put into it each year, the better the result."

"That's a good metaphor for life, James. How's that speech coming on? I know you're a perfectionist, but I am going to get a look at it before tomorrow, aren't I?"

"I think it's done. I'll have another look later and then you can have it. I'm…I'm going to take these roses to Mrs Samuel."

Offering a wave to all the residents who greeted him from their chairs, James headed down the corridor. Cliff, who was in one of the rooms and reading a book to a man lying in bed, peered over his glasses at James as he passed.

"Now, James. Don't they look something special," gesturing at the roses. "I know a lady who might like those."

"I'm…I'm on my way to her room now. Is she there?"

Cliff gave a little salute to confirm she was.

Arriving at Mrs Samuel's doorway, James saw a familiar pair of polished brown shoes and smart trousers sticking out and his heart sank. John Samuel was on the edge of the bed, leaning forward with his elbows on his knees, typing something on his phone, tutting. The communication clearly wasn't pleasing him. Mrs Samuel was in her chair staring at the floor, both her hands were gripping the arms of the chair. James walked in and John didn't even bother trying to hide the sigh as he glanced at him. Gutted that John was there, James stepped over his outstretched legs and sat down on the bed next to Mrs Samuel, placing the flowers next to him. John tinkered with his phone and James did all he could to ignore his presence.

"Hello… hi… Mrs Samuel?"

Mrs Samuel's gaze didn't move from the floor and James felt disheartened. He wanted to walk out and come back later when John had gone. He could be himself then – he hated the way John made him feel.

"I've had nothing out of her today. Not a thing," said John, enlarging something on his screen that looked like a graph and squinting at it.

James cleared his throat and tried again: "Mrs Samuel? It's James. James?"

"I honestly don't know why you're bothering," John cut in.

"The churchyard boy. The flower boy. The boy with the flowers. The roses," James continued.

Mrs Samuel remained completely passive. Remembering he actually *had* roses with him, James thrust them forward.

"Flowers. I've bought you some flowers, Mrs Samuel. Roses. Harry's roses. For you. Julia's Rose. They've bloomed again. In my garden."

The sound of John tapping his phone had stopped and James felt his eyes on him. He wanted to run away – but ever so slowly, Mrs Samuel's eyes refocused and tracked across the room, gradually making their way towards James until she had lifted her head. Staring him directly in the eye, her expression didn't change.

"Look," James said, persisting, tilting the bunch forward. "It's your roses, Mrs Samuel. The ones Harry used to grow for you. Julia's Rose. I grow them now, for you – and for Harry."

James thought he noticed a slight flicker in Mrs Samuel's eyes and it spurred him on. Sliding the golden rose out from the middle of the bunch, James held Mrs

Samuel's hand and turned it, placing it in her grasp. He closed her fingers around the stem. Her eyes moved from James's face to the rose. Cliff appeared at the door.

"Just checking all is ok, Julia? Am I ok to come in?" he said, looking at John.

"The more the merrier. Why not? I spend my life packed in here like a sardine, so another one won't make much difference. Anyone else out there we can invite in to join us?" John replied, dramatically peering into the corridor.

"Good, good," Cliff said, ignoring John with a wry smile. "Oh, Julia. Just look at those flowers. You're a lucky lady today."

Cliff filled Mrs Samuel's cup up from the jug then straightened some of the items on top of the drawers. John went back to his phone. James watched Mrs Samuel, who was staring at the rose. Moving it higher, she clasped the rose tightly with both hands. She began to mumble and James leaned closer trying to catch what she was saying. She was muttering something, and then James realised – she was singing. She was singing a song. Her voice was dry and a little croaky, but she sang louder and the song was clearer – a beautiful melody about green trees and red roses. Cliff spun round with the widest of smiles and joined in, flinging his arms in the air with delight and singing along with her. He plonked himself down next to James, budging John's legs out of the way with a waft of his hand causing James and John to bounce up and down. The three of them were now perched on the bed.

"Ahhhh, 'What a Wonderful World', Julia, a Louis Armstrong song - one of my favourites. Second verse, come on, I bet you know it". He reached forward and patted Mrs Samuel's elbow and looked into her eyes and led the singing of the next verse.

The amazing thing was, she *did* know it, and she sang along softly. From behind them, a voice joined in on the last line, *"...what a wonderful world"* – it was John Samuel, his voice cracking. Cliff and James turned in surprise to see a tear trickling down John's cheek. He smiled sadly. It struck James that he had never seen John smile, let alone through tears.

"Harry, Dad, used to sing that song around the house. I remember now. Sometimes he would hold Mum in his arms and they would dance in the kitchen as he sang," he said, wiping his eyes with his forearm. "And Mum would sing it to me when I was a child, at bedtime, or when I'd had a bad day. She was always there when I was upset, always knew how to make it better. She was a good mum, one of the best. They were both great parents." Sniffing, John slipped his phone into his pocket and got up off the bed. "Come on Mum, let's put those lovely roses in a vase for you. Cliff can't sit round here all day singing, he's got a job to do. And James..." James waited for a withering comment. "…well, James has got a legal case with the Parish Council to go and win."

Cliff heaved himself up off the bed. "It was the golden rose, James. The golden rose – it helped her remember her song!"

John took the bunch of roses from James and went to take the single rose from Mrs Samuel's grasp, thought better of it and rubbed her hand gently instead.

"John, can we see Harry? His birthday is next week."

John opened his mouth to say something, stopped himself, then crouched down in front of her.

"Mum, Dad died remember? We can't see him anymore. I'm really sorry."

She rolled her eyes.

"I know that, you daft donut. I'm not completely doolally. I want to visit his grave on his birthday!"

Chapter 25

That evening, James sat at the desk in in his bedroom studying his speech. Paul had advised him to keep it short and concise, no waffle. Know want you want to say, say it firmly, but keep it polite. James checked Mr Adamson's notes one last time to make sure he hadn't missed any important details. Just before bedtime, Paul knocked and stuck his head around the door.

"Nearly time for sleep, Champ. Are you ready for me to give it a quick once over? I could do with a heads up on what I'm saying."

James nodded and Paul took the paper and read through it, umming and nodding a few times.

"Very good, James. I would just… it's a bit… no, you know what? It's great. They have to listen to this. No matter what they decide, you've done everything you can."

He sat down on James's bed and ruffled his hair. James shook his fringe back into place. He wondered why *everyone* kept doing that.

"I wish I could do the speech," James said. "I wish I

could just stand up and do it. I just want to be a bit more…
a bit more… like someone who could do something like
that."

"Don't be daft, James. We live in a world where
confidence is celebrated and being quiet and shy can
mean people don't get the recognition they deserve. Come
on, get ready for bed – big day tomorrow."

Waking early, James felt sick. His tummy churned and
his visits to the toilet went off the chart. The school day
dragged. He doubted whether anyone else was even aware
of the plight of the gravestones, and they certainly wouldn't
have known it was all James thought about that day. After
a quick tea, which he poked at but didn't really feel like
eating, James and Paul walked to the Village Hall together
in the evening sunshine – aeroplane trails cut across the
orangey blue sky. Paul had James's speech tucked into his
jacket pocket and James clutched Mr Adamson's notes so
he had them to refer to if needed. It felt like Mr Adamson
was at least partly with them after all the work he had put
in. Crossing the car park, James noticed a familiar figure
sitting on the bench in the churchyard. As usual, James
had insisted they left the house with plenty of time to
spare.

"Dad, can I nip and see Reverend Varga? She's over
there, in the churchyard."

"I don't see why not, James," Paul replied, waving
over to her. She waved back with a double-handed wave.
"It'll give me a chance to read this speech through one
more time."

Paul sat down on one of the benches under the lychgate roof and James made his way up the path to Reverend Varga, who was beaming at him. He hadn't seen her for ages.

"You are here for the meeting, no?" she asked as he sat down next to her.

"Yes. I don't want them to get rid of the gravestones. They are too important. I think it's…it's silly they can't see that," James said.

Reverend Varga chuckled. "Make sure you say it in the meeting. You shall be seeing me there shortly, I am on the panel."

James was incredulous.

"You are on the panel? Are you cross with me for trying to stop the decision?"

"Cross because you are passionate about your village's churchyard? Cross because you want to fight for what you believe? Heavens, no. The Parish Council are my employers so I must listen to their concerns. I shall be taking in any other views too, no problem. Are you ok speaking?"

James shook his head and looked at the floor.

"I can't. My dad is doing it. I wrote what I want him to say. Mr Adamson from the care home helped me."

"This is good. Remember this James, my friend, without fear there can't be courage. Come on, let's go and get this done with."

The Village Hall was a black and white timber building, commonplace in the area where James lived. Inside, there were some rows of plastic chairs set out with a handful

of people sitting down. The floorboards were of polished wood which gleamed as the evening sun shone through the Georgian windows. The chairs faced a table at the front of the hall, the kind with legs that folded down so they could be stored away easily. Reverend Varga was greeting three other people who were already sitting down facing the audience. She pulled up a chair and squeezed at the end of the table. There was a gentleman who James immediately recognised, with two women either side. When James was in Year 6, he had visited the churchyard and been shocked by some graffiti he found on a gravestone. Bending down to try to rub it off, the man who was sitting at the front of the hall had appeared, shouting at James. He blamed James and called him a hooligan. James presumed he must be in charge of the meeting because he was sitting in the middle of the table and had the air of someone trying to look important. He was wearing grey trousers and a blue blazer with gold buttons, over a checked shirt. Sitting forward with his hands clasped on the desk in front of him, he peered over the top of a pair of half-moon glasses with beady eyes. The top of his head was bald and shiny and the hair which remained looked a suspicious brown colour for someone his age.

"That's Mr Fossington-Smythe, the Chairman of the Parish Council," whispered Paul, leaning in. "He's been in charge for about thirty years. He's a bit of a pompous old dinosaur and always thinks he knows best. He must be in his eighties now. The two ladies either side are his deputies I think."

Mr Fossington-Smythe cleared his throat and spoke.

"Right, well, it's 7pm. Let's proceed with the meeting. Our treasurer, Mrs Fitzgerald, here to my right will be taking minutes. Mrs Farquhar on my left is Deputy Chairman, and Reverend Varga will be no stranger to you, I'm sure. There are a couple of routine items on the agenda, the floor will then be open to consultation regarding the removal of the *dangerous* gravestones in the churchyard." He already sounded affronted that anyone would even question his decision to remove them. In the hall there were five rows of eight chairs. Only forty seats, but they were only just over a quarter full. James counted thirteen people in attendance, including him and Paul. His petition had only attracted forty-two signatures and he almost wondered why he was bothering if no one else in the village cared about its history. He had forwarded it on to the Parish Council anyway, but he was disheartened.

Mr Fossington-Smythe went through his agenda items, discussing the appointment of a new contractor to cut the churchyard grass. He tutted about the expensive replacement of one of the stained glass window panels and discussed a few other issues. Mrs Fitzgerald read through the latest accounts in a near whisper and it was all so mundane, James almost forgot why they were there. In fact, he could have quite easily dozed off in the musty hall.

"Now, agenda item six," announced Mr Fossington-Smythe solemnly, pausing and glaring around the room over his glasses, "the removal of the derelict gravestones in the churchyard. Our position is clear – Mr Brassley, the church groundskeeper, and I have spent considerable time assessing each gravestone. It is our opinion that a number of the gravestones are a falling hazard and we have a duty of care to anyone visiting the churchyard, as per the official guidance."

He waved a thick document in the air with a flourish. It was the guidance notes that Mr Adamson had pored over.

"You are probably not aware but we have to adhere to strict guidance, and it states that we must ensure that people who visit the churchyard are not subjected to the risk of falling headstones. We've taken note of the petition in the village and, how should I say it, the rather *underwhelming* response. We've detailed our decision on the Parish Council website which I am sure you have all taken the time to absorb. Any questions, or can we move on to the next item? Good. Now, item seven, the tiling on the lychgate…"

Noticing Reverend Varga raise her eyebrows at him, James sat up and nudged Paul.

"Dad, I think that was your chance to speak," he hissed.

"Oh, yes, I see, righty-ho, here we go then," Paul whispered back. He coughed and put his hand up. "Yes, hello, over here. We have a few points to make about the gravestones. Well, more my son, James here – he's written some notes and would like me to read them out."

Mr Fossington-Smythe sighed wearily and motioned for Paul to stand. Reverend Varga put her elbow on the table and her hand up to her mouth to hide a smile. Paul stood up and unfolded the notes shakily, as others in the hall turned to look at him. Voice wobbling, he started speaking.

"Yes, right, thank you. James has spent some time exploring the guidance and also sought the legal advice of a… erm… friend." Mr Fossington-Smythe rolled his eyes. Paul coughed again. "Yes, well, anyway, here are James's views."

He shook the notes again.

"I understand that the Parish Council has a duty of care to people visiting the churchyard. I know the Parish Council has to assess the risks and do what it can to minimise them. However, the legal guidance you follow says that it must be a proportionate approach to managing risk. I do not think that removing the gravestones is proportionate." A blotchy red rash started spreading up Mr Fossington-Smythe's neck and he rearranged his tie. He was the only member of the panel who didn't look at Paul as he spoke.

"Firstly, the gravestones do not belong to the church or the Parish Council. In order to remove a gravestone, the Parish Council must take all reasonable steps to contact the family of the deceased and seek permission. Can the

Parish Council say it has done this?" Paul glanced up at the committee panel. Mr Fossington-Smythe tapped his gold pen on the pad in front of him.

"Secondly, a gravestone can only be removed if it is about to collapse imminently, I am not convinced this is the case. If you do believe this to be the case, under section 7 of the guidance, you should have instructed a specialist structural engineer to assess the risks and provide a report. Section 8 of the guidance states that due to historical value, the church can still decide not to remove the gravestone even if it is a risk, it might be more appropriate to carry out maintenance. Can you provide evidence that this has been considered?"

Paul paused again. Mr Fossington-Smythe took a sip of water and it caught in his throat causing him to splutter a number of times and turn the colour of a beetroot. Finding his feet now, James felt Paul's presence growing and his voice sounding steelier.

"The guidance is clear – before removing a gravestone, the church has an obligation to do all it can to preserve it. There are a number of alternative options that should be considered: the gravestone could have a warning placed nearby; they could have a low fence built around them to ensure no one can get close; gravestones can be reset into the ground. Finally, a taller gravestone can be reinforced."

Mr Fossington-Smythe put up his hand to stop Paul, as if to say 'enough is enough'. Looking directly at James, he narrowed his already narrow eyes further.

"Young man, I understand this is important to you, I really do. But in your innocence there are issues here that you are failing to grasp. We are a parish council, *not* a school council. Everything you have suggested would be wonderful in an *ideal* world. In the *real* world we simply do not have the finances to even consider your proposals – these are specialist jobs. Unless *you* yourself have the money to donate, of course?"

James squirmed in his seat as he thought about Paul's recent financial worries. Anger rose within him and the pulse in his temple throbbed. He wanted to scream at Mr Fossington-Smythe that he was a fuddy-duddy old man who couldn't see past the end of his own, considerably large, nose. But he didn't, he remembered a note Mr Adamson had written at the end of the document.

More than anything when presenting a case, talk about how it makes you feel. How does it make you feel losing the gravestones? Talking about feelings is far more powerful that any legal jargon and it's feelings that often win cases.

Before James knew it, he found himself standing up looking at all the faces turned in his direction. His legs wobbled. Mr Fossington-Smythe continued to stare at him with his piercing eyes, beneath his bushy grey eyebrows which didn't match the colour of his hair. James opened his mouth to speak, but nothing came.

"Yes, well, if that's everything. Now, back to item seven," Mr Fossington-Smythe said dismissively.

James sat down again and hung his head. Paul patted his leg and it felt like an acceptance of defeat. James lifted his head again and saw a combative look on Reverend Varga's face – *without fear there can't be courage.* Mr Fossington-Smythe was discussing a loose tile on the lychgate. James stood up again.

"Wait... wait... I want to say... I mean, I just need to say... please don't move the gravestones." He paused, realising that this probably wasn't the strongest argument he could have mustered and Mr Fossington-Smythe sighed another deep, contemptuous sigh. James took a deep breath. "I mean... they are too important. They... well... they are probably the only thing left to remind us of those villagers. They are the only reminder that they lived here in this village. It's hundreds of years of history you are wiping out – people's histories, familys histories, the *village's* history. A churchyard is the starting place where people can learn about their local area's history. It... it was for me, thanks to Mrs Samuel. We have a responsibility to this history and we have to respect it, even if... even if it costs us a bit more money. The people deserve to be remembered. The families of those people deserve to have them remembered. Without them we... we wouldn't have this lovely village."

With his heart pounding, James took a deep breath and realised the faces around him were now smiling. One old lady performed a little mimed clap in his direction. James plonked himself down again and there was a murmur of chatter in the hall. Paul put his arm around him and hugged him.

"Wow, I've never seen you like that before. Good on you, Champ!"

Mr Fossington-Smythe seemed to berate his Deputy who had whispered something in his ear and Reverend Varga was writing notes. The mouse-like lady taking the minutes continued to type at a panicky speed without looking up. Now puce, Mr Fossington-Smythe turned back to James and boomed at him.

"Yes, yes, that's all very well, all very well I'm sure. But I can only repeat, young man, we do not have the money. It would cost thousands of pounds extra to even contemplate…"

"How many thousands?" a loud voice cut him off and Mr Fossington-Smythe shot a thunderous look beyond James to the back of the hall. "How many thousands? You haven't said. Get a quote and I will pay."

There was excited chatter in the hall again and James and Paul turned simultaneously to see John Samuel standing at the back of the hall. Mr Fossington-Smythe's mouth was wide open like a goldfish, completely unable to say anything, and it was the most satisfying thing James had ever seen.

Chapter 26

James wished there was another route to get to the church. Ahead, five or six girls were crowding around the bench outside the shops, sharing phones and cackling at something on the screens. James was heartened to see Malika's topknot sticking out above the group. In a small village, he could always guarantee when he didn't want to be seen, he'd be seen by *everybody* – even on a Thursday evening. For a start he was baking in his hoodie. He didn't like taking it off so he had to put up with feeling uncomfortably warm. He was also carrying a bucket with a number of cleaning utensils inside – a cloth, a soft bristle brush, some polish, a roll of masking tape and a pair of scissors. To top it off, he'd wedged a bunch of roses in there too and they were sticking out.

"Do you only have a *pink* bucket?" James had asked his mum before he left.

"Sorry James, I didn't really consider which bucket colour is the most fashionable when I picked one up from ASDA," she'd replied.

Fixing his eyes to the floor, James hoped the girls wouldn't notice him.

"James! Hi!" called Malika as he walked by. His heart skipped a beat as he realised he had no other option than to stop. He tried to keep his eye contact fixed on Malika and ignore the other girls who had gone silent and were eyeing his worn hoodie, too small jeans and his bucket. There was a collective look of thinly disguised disgust on their faces. Desperately trying to hold his gaze on Malika's eyes, he started to worry that this was giving her the impression that he was being a bit intense, so he averted his gaze back to the floor. It was no wonder he could barely speak to anyone when he was concentrating so hard on what to do with his eyes.

"What are you up to?" Malika asked brightly. She was genuinely taking an interest and James respected the fact she was also ignoring the looks on her friends' faces and that she was giving him the time of day. James flicked his fringe out of his face.

"I'm erm, nothing really, just… you know…," he realised they really wouldn't know. Literally no other twelve year old would be carrying a pink bucket, complete with cleaning utensils and roses, through the village – ever. This conversation would be something he would be cringing about for days and there was no way to rescue it.

"I… I better be going," he said after an excruciating moment.

There were a few snorts and giggles behind him. When he got to the end of the shops, he heard Malika again.

"James! James, wait!" she called, and he turned to

see her jogging up behind him. "Sorry, I know you hate situations like that. It was just nice to see you. I said hello without thinking. What *are* you doing with that pink bucket?" she grinned.

"I'm… I'm going to clean Harry's grave – Mrs Samuel's husband. She's in a care home now and she can't get to see it. Her son has finally agreed to take her up there on Saturday afternoon because it was his birthday on that date. Harry, I mean. We're going at 2pm, just like she always used to. It's… it's a bit of a mess up there, they haven't even cut the grass for weeks, but I'm going to do my best with Harry's grave, just like *she* used to. She worries everyone has forgotten him, and her. I want her, them, to feel… thought about."

"That's really nice, James. I'm sure she'll like it." Malika looked behind her and James could see the girls watching them, arms folded. They looked less threatening somehow – their main source of confidence, Malika, was with him.

"I better go, James," Malika took a step to leave then hesitated. "You know what makes you speak the most, James? The times when you really open up?" James shrugged.

"It's your kindness, James. You're very kind. See you soon!"

Watching her return to the girls, James saw their relief as Malika positioned herself back in the middle of the group. The laughing resumed. He saw Malika reach for her phone from her pocket and start tapping away.

Along the main road to the church there were some temporary traffic lights in place as the council finally appeared to be fixing the potholes in the road and a long queue of cars were waiting for the green light. James hated walking past a line of cars. He felt like every car occupant was looking at him and he self-consciously turned his body away from the road towards the hedge as he walked.

Except for the cawing sound of the crows warning of James's presence, the churchyard was quiet. James filled his bucket with some water from an outside tap, squirted in some detergent and scrubbed the moss away from the engraving on Harry's grave. He thought back to how he used to watch Mrs Samuel tend to the grave. He would be her assistant, passing her a number of different cleaning implements she would request from the bag on her walking frame. He trimmed the grass around the base of the gravestone and sprayed some Windowlene onto the marble and polished it until it was shiny. He wiped over the little ornamental bird and changed the masking tape. In over a year, neither he nor Mrs Samuel had ever managed to get it to stand up straight. It was important it was there though, for Mrs Samuel.

Some of the older gravestones had warning tape around them to signify maintenance work was taking place and James was delighted. John Samuel had obviously put his money where his mouth was. James smiled to himself at the thought of Mr Fossington-Smythe having to organise all the work he didn't want to happen. James despaired at the long, unkempt grass though. There was nothing he could do about it so he concentrated on making Harry's grave look tidy for Mrs Samuel on Saturday. That was his priority. His last job was to place his bunch of Julia's Roses in the

little ceramic vase at the base of the gravestone. The weather forecast was for fine weather so he was sure they would be ok for a couple of days.

Saturday came and James felt a feeling of melancholy he couldn't quite put into words. This wasn't unusual – he would often get stuck in this mood. Random, but very vivid flashbacks of the past often made him feel a strange sadness that he couldn't put into words. Taking Mrs Samuel to the churchyard was something he desperately wanted to happen, but it also reminded him how she could no longer get there by herself and he missed meeting her there at 2pm each Saturday. At 1.30pm, James went into the lounge to say goodbye to his parents. Jessie was sitting on a little red push car and she came trundling over and rammed into his trainers.

"I'm going now, Jessie," he said picking her up.

"Jay, Jay churcha. Churcha!" she said patting his head.

"That's right Jessie, I'm going up to the church with Mrs Samuel today. How did you…?"

"It's amazing what they pick up just listening to conversations going on around them," said Paul quickly. "She's really coming on isn't she?"

James was secretly glad Jessie was out of the baby stage – he was never quite sure what to do with her and had hated all the piercing crying and not being able to know for sure what was wrong with her. Jessie still cried sometimes, but it was now much easier to work out what she needed.

"I'll see you later," James said.

"Everything ok, love? You're not worried about going with John are you? We've been in touch with him and he seems quite happy about it all. Or as happy as John Samuel ever is," she said with a shrug. "Anyway, we're only a text away."

James was nervous about being in John's company but he'd do whatever it took for Mrs Samuel. He usually worried about what he would say but John was so disinterested, it didn't seem to matter.

"I'm ok. I think," James said. "I don't know, I always get stuck thinking about the past so much, but I'm only twelve. I don't have much past. Mrs Samuel, she has eighty-three years of memories. All those memories of Harry – she must want to turn the clock back and be back in that time with him."

"Yep, time is a funny thing," said Paul. "We'd all like to pause it sometimes, or turn it backwards. Occasionally we want to fast-forward too! Memories can make us happy though, they don't have to make us sad."

"You're doing a nice thing today, love," said Sally. "I'm sure she'll appreciate it."

James was relieved there was no one from his school around for a change as he wandered to the top of the village. John's huge black car was in the care home car park – a sight which always made James's tummy lurch.

Laura and Cliff were nowhere to be seen and a member of staff he didn't know very well let him in. James peered into Mr Adamson's room to say hello – his bed was made and his chair was empty. When James arrived at Mrs Samuel's doorway, he saw John Samuel sitting on the bed. Mrs Samuel was sitting in the chair.

"Oh hello, John. You came!" Mrs Samuel beamed from the chair. She was wearing chequered trousers, black shoes and a smart navy coat.

"Alright?" John muttered in James's direction, then to Mrs Samuel: "He's James and I'm John, Mum. Confusing, I know."

Waiting for John to finish doing whatever he was doing on his phone, James stood there not really sure what to do. He began to doubt that they'd arranged to take Mrs Samuel anywhere at all.

"What day is it?" asked Mrs Samuel. "Are we doing anything nice?"

"Right," said John abruptly, clicking off his phone and standing up. "Laura has let us borrow a wheelchair." He pointed at a folded up wheelchair by the door. He and James wrestled with it for a minute or two, trying to open it out.

"Are we going somewhere nice?" Mrs Samuel asked again brightly.

"We're going to see Harry's grave," replied James. "It was his birthday on this date, Mrs Samuel."

"Harry?" said Mrs Samuel. "Why, he only visited a few hours ago."

"No…no, Mrs Samuel. It's Saturday, 2pm, your time to visit Harry's grave."

Mrs Samuel's eyes lit up and she sat forward. "We need flowers, flowers from that shop – the one in the village. Where's my walker? I'll need my walker."

"I've… I've sorted your flowers, don't worry," James said.

"You don't need your walker today, Mum," said John breathlessly as he finally got the wheelchair unfolded and clicked into place. "We've not just spent the past ten minutes trying to get this thing up for nothing."

When Mrs Samuel was comfortable in her wheelchair, John wheeled her to the car. After helping her into the front seat and putting her seatbelt on, John slammed her door and then put the wheelchair in the boot. James got in the back seat – it was shiny cream leather. John pulled out of the car park and onto the main road. Not wanting to in some way scuff the pristine seat, James didn't dare move. The car was furnished with dark polished wood and hardly made a sound as they glided down the road. Mrs Samuel gazed out of the window with a look of wonder on her face, as if she'd never seen the outside world. She watched as they passed the village green and the shops.

"You used to play on that field, didn't you John?" she said, then she spied the church tower rising above the trees in the distance. "We're going to the churchyard aren't we?"

"It wasn't really a big secret, was it? We've been telling you where we're going all week," said John, glancing at James in the mirror and rolling his eyes upwards. James smiled.

Chapter 27

Standing at the top of the path in the shadow of the church, Malika checked the clock on the church tower. Next to her was Tom, on his crutches. Mr Ramos, Mrs Shah, Reverend Varga, Laura and Cliff all stood in a row with them. Cliff was holding on to the handles of a wheelchair, and in it sat Mr Adamson proudly dressed in his tweed suit with his pocket watch attached to the waistcoat. Next to Cliff were James's parents – Paul was holding Jessie. In front of them, lining either side of the path down to the lychgate were pupils from the school; Malika's friends, and a handful of Tom's – including Josh. They were chatting and laughing to each other across the path. The graveyard had been freshly mowed that morning. There were still grass clippings everywhere, but Malika was glad it had been mowed at short notice.

Eventually a black car turned between the hedges at the entrance to the Village Hall car park and crunched across the gravel. Malika saw the glare of the sun on the windscreen and John Samuel pull the sun visor down.

"Here we go, they're here!" called Malika. There were a few shushes and everyone fell quiet, except for Jessie, who was loudly pointing out the crows to Paul. The car came to a stop just to the right of the lychgate. Malika saw John Samuel turn and say something to James and James ducked down to peer at everyone waiting. He had anxiety written over his face. Malika knew the surprise would send James into a spin, but she balanced that with the hope that he would appreciate what she had organised for Mrs Samuel.

John got out the car and self-consciously removed the wheelchair from the boot and took it round to Mrs Samuel's door and helped her into it. James got out as well and he was trying not to look up at everyone. John started pushing Mrs Samuel towards the lychgate and onto the cobbles beneath. Hidden behind them, James seemed comfortable to be following. When they were underneath the lychgate John stopped, turned and said something to James. James shook his head. Mrs Samuel craned back and said something too and John gestured again at the wheelchair to James. The children waiting on the path looked across at each other and shrugged and there was a little murmur from the row of people waiting with Malika. She hoped she hadn't expected too much of James. Hesitating, he stepped forward and took the handles of Mrs Samuel's wheelchair and John stood behind them, their roles reversed. James starting pushing and as they emerged from the lychgate a little cheer went up from the waiting guard of honour. Mrs Samuel smiled from ear to ear. James didn't take his eyes off Malika at the top of the path as he pushed Mrs Samuel between his clapping peers. She was his focus, he could blank everything out if he focused on her.

Reverend Varga bobbed her head forward, "Have you done this for Mrs Samuel or James, Malika?"

Malika giggled, "Maybe a bit of both!"

"She thinks she's the Queen!" said Mr Ramos, as they all watched Mrs Samuel waving regally to the children on either side of the path.

"What do we do when they are reaching the grave?" asked Reverend Varga as they all looked on.

"We need a speech of course," barked Mr Adamson from his wheelchair. He turned to speak to Malika but struggled to crane his head forward to see her at the end of the row which made him sound even more irritable. "Young lady, you need to address everyone and say why we are all here."

Laura reached over and rearranged Mr Adamson's blanket, which had become untucked.

"That's quite a big thing for a young girl to do, Mr Adamson," she said.

"It's not that, it's just that I don't really know how to explain why we're here," said Malika, in a matter-of-fact tone.

"Oh, great," said Mr Ramos in mock-seriousness. "You mean I'm missing the football and you don't even know why we're here. I wish he'd hurry up with that wheelchair, I might be able to catch the second half. For someone who has just run the school record for the 1500m, he's taking his time. He'd best not strain a muscle either, we've got the County Championship cross country on Wednesday night. I'm banking on him – we never usually get a sniff of a podium finish. He's the best prospect I've seen for a long time."

Mr Ramos looked down the row and stuck his thumb up at Paul and Sally who smiled proudly.

"Hey, John Samuel works in computers doesn't he? I wonder if he's got any work going?" whispered Paul, bending down to Sally.

"Paul! I can't believe you're thinking of yourself at a time like this," replied Sally.

"Oh yes, of course, sorry," said Paul sheepishly, standing upright again.

"Besides, I've already sent him a message," whispered Sally. "He said he's going to ring you on Monday about a contract he needs the right person for."

Paul grinned and kissed her on the cheek, and they watched Mrs Samuel point at the little bird on top of Harry's grave and say something to James. James nodded and pushed the wheelchair a little further then stopped and applied the brake.

Stepping forward, John helped Mrs Samuel out of her chair. He held her by the arm for a moment while she steadied herself. They shuffled across the grass with John holding tightly, until they were in front of Harry's grave. They stood a moment, looking down. John handed Mrs Samuel a tissue and she dabbed her eyes. In silence, the children joined the adults at the top of the path and James followed. He stood by his parents and Paul put his arm around him and squeezed his shoulder.

"Jay, Jay. Ms Sam Sam," Jessie called.

"That's right Jessie, James helped Mrs Samuel," Sally whispered.

"So what *do* we do now?" Mr Ramos whispered loudly.

"Well, after a few failed attempts in the care home kitchen late last night, Laura and I made a birthday cake to celebrate Harry and his birthday. There's enough for everyone to have a little piece, and some drinks," said Cliff, thumbing behind him to some Tupperware boxes and plastic cups.

"But we *need* a speech!" hissed Mr Adamson.

"I think you *can* tell everyone why we're here, Malika, can't you?" said Mrs Shah, smiling encouragingly.

"Well I suppose I know how much Mrs Samuel and Harry did for the village, they deserve our recognition. I know how much they have done because James has told me. It means a lot to James that we say thank you to people who have served the village so well. It's the one thing he can talk about freely and passionately, and I lo… like him

166

for that. We're here to say thank you to Mrs Samuel, and James, and to remember Harry on his birthday."

The row all went silent for a moment and Sally squeezed Paul's hand. Through his awkwardness and shyness, Malika saw the good in James.

"Oh good heavens, girl," Mr Adamson exclaimed. "That was your speech. It was perfect. Just say *that*!"

Chapter 28

The adults were making small talk and drinking from the plastic cups. The children were on the grass eating Cliff and Laura's cake. They chatted happily in the late afternoon sun. Sitting on the bench were James, Tom and Malika. James listened to Malika and Tom as they discussed Malika's organisational skills, and how her mum and dad had helped her to contact just about anyone she could think of who had anything to do with James and Mrs Samuel. Using her powers of persuasion, they had all agreed to join them at the churchyard. They giggled at how it had taken Malika's mum half an hour to persuade the abrupt old man at the Parish Council to arrange for the grass to be cut for the occasion. Looking out over the village, his village, James felt a rare feeling of contentedness. In front of him, Mrs Samuel and Mr Adamson were facing each other in their wheelchairs, eating cake. Standing nearby, Laura and Cliff were chatting with his parents. Jessie was toddling back and to, entertaining some of Malika's friends who were squealing about how cute she was.

"Malika?" James said. "I… I just… thank you. Thank you for today."

Malika laughed and reached over and hugged him. Sally glanced over and smiled which made James blush.

"The thing is, James. You're the shyest person I know, right? But over the last few months, you've shown just about everyone how to be confident. You might not do it in a loud way, but you've done stuff most outgoing people would struggle with. You just don't see it."

She laughed and looked at Tom who nodded.

"That's not the only thing he doesn't see," said Tom, nudging Malika. She punched him on the arm playfully in return.

"It's actually true what she's saying though, mate. It must be all those roses you grow, flower boy. They must give you some kind of *flower power!*" Tom said, smiling. "Look, James, that thing with the pear. I really regret that. I'm sorry. It was horrible and I was pretty shocked when it happened. I was worried about making friends at high school and I guess I went along with it to keep *him* happy." Tom stretched his leg out to point a toe in Josh's direction, and grimaced as he forgot he shouldn't be moving his knee. "I told him afterwards, I told him it was wrong. I made sure he was here today too, to show some respect."

The three of them watched John Samuel say something to Cliff and Laura, then bend down and speak to Mrs Samuel. He took the handles of Mrs Samuel's wheelchair and released the brake with his foot. Nodding at James, Malika and Tom, he started pushing her towards the path.

"That's a bit rude. He doesn't even say goodbye?" said Malika, tutting.

"He still doesn't give us the time of day, after everything," said Tom.

"I don't know," said James. "I think he might just be a bit quiet – a bit shy. Sometimes that can come across as rude."

Malika shrugged.

"I just want to… I'm just going to see them," said James, getting up. John and Mrs Samuel were already half-way down the path. Mrs Samuel turned her head slowly as they passed Harry's grave.

"I'm just going to say goodbye," James said, as he passed his parents.

"Ok, love," replied Sally. "You'll have to be quick to catch them."

As James hurried towards the path, Mr Adamson grabbed his wrist.

"Hey, lad, we really showed them didn't we?" Mr Adamson pointed at the graves where work was in progress. "They had nowhere to turn with our legal know-how – there'll be a place for you at my firm when you're old enough, no doubt about that."

"Thank you, Mr Adamson. I… I'm so happy they listened to us and that John helped too. Thank you for everything you did."

James watched as John wheeled Mrs Samuel under the lychgate and towards the car.

"You mark my words, lad, if they ever try anything like that…"

"Mr Adamson," James said, "I'm going to have to go. I'm going to say goodbye to Mrs Samuel."

"Oh of course lad, you must. She's a fine lady is Julia."

James jogged down the path and under the lychgate. John was just about to help Mrs Samuel out of the wheelchair onto the front seat. The car door was open and she had her back to him.

"Wait! I just want… I need to speak to Mrs Samuel."

"Ok, but she's looking tired," said John. "It's been a long day."

He stood back and James went round to the front of Mrs Samuel and crouched down.

"Mrs Samuel, I just wanted to say goodbye. I hope you enjoyed your day. Malika, my friend, organised it and it was a surprise to me too. We wanted to show you that Harry isn't forgotten, and that you… you… are special to people."

Mrs Samuel stared straight ahead, over James's shoulder, across the playing field to the bowling green in the distance where Harry had played each Friday night for decades. James knew that look, but he was relieved she'd had a 'good day' and she had been to see Harry's grave as she wanted. James patted her hand and stood up.

"Bye," he said to John.

"Yeah, see you," said John.

"Thank you, John. For… for…" James said.

"No probs," replied John, before James could finish.

James started to head back to the group, hands in pockets.

"Son? son?" Mrs Samuel suddenly called, trying to

look behind her. James stopped and spun round. John shrugged and turned her wheelchair to face James.

Mrs Samuel took a moment, gathering her thoughts.

"I have lots of memories of Harry. They are all up here, somewhere." She tapped her head. "They're getting a bit muddled, mind. But today, you and your friends have created *new* memories for me. Happy memories, and I'll treasure them. Thank you, son. And thank you to everyone."

James smiled – a wide, happy smile.

"I'll see you soon, Mrs Samuel. Next Saturday, 2pm," James said, "on the dot."

Chapter 29

James was playing with Jessie in the garden. Paul and Sally were sitting at the patio table – Paul was working on his laptop and whistling a lively tune and Sally was reading a book. James was kicking a ball to Jessie and laughing at her attempts to kick it back. She would crouch down unsteadily and stop it with both hands. Lining up her foot, she would take a swing and miss, falling backwards onto her nappy-cushioned bottom.

"We should take a photo of you with your trophy and send it to Jeremy and Denise," said Sally, peering over her book.

James hated having his picture taken.

"Mr Ramos said it should be in the school newsletter next week. They'll probably want to mention it in assembly," Sally continued.

"Hmm," said James, frowning. He wondered if winning the County Cross Country Championship was worth the stress of having the spotlight on him.

"I'll let them know you don't want that, James," said

Sally, reading his mind. "You won, and you should be able to enjoy it and not have any worries to detract from it."

The doorbell rang inside the house.

"I'll go," James said and headed for the patio door. Jessie screamed in disgust that he had dared to end their game. Once anyone started playing with Jessie, she rarely let them leave without a fight.

"I'll be back in a minute, Jessie. Look," he went back and placed the ball by her foot, "you have a kick and I'll be straight back."

James wandered through the house to the front door. He peeked through the eye hole but no one was there. He opened the door and looked both ways – then down. On the doormat was a heavy duty cardboard box with a lid on. It was the kind of box that looked like it once held important files or documents – one that would usually be found stored in a loft or garage. It had his name scrawled on the top in black marker pen.

James reached down to pick it up by the handles – it was heavy, heavier than he was expecting. Groaning as his back took the strain, he staggered back down the hall, shoving the door shut with a backward kick. Struggling through the doors to the patio, he thumped the box onto the table.

"What the…?" Paul said, looking up from his laptop. "You scared the life out of me. Where on earth has that come from?"

"It was at the door. I don't know what it is. It's got my name on it."

"Well open the lid, but be careful," said Sally, frowning.

No one was really sure why James needed to be careful, but it added to the drama as he eased the lid off. Jessie was now running after a butterfly, shrieking. James placed the lid on the patio table and peered in. There was a hastily written note on a business compliment slip at the top:

To James,

I thought you'd appreciate these more than me. I know Mum would be far happier knowing you were caring for them. I'll see you soon at the care home. Cliff won't be there for a while unfortunately, I've helped him organise a visit home to his family.

Thanks for everything you have done for Mum.

John

Beneath the note, James saw the image of Elvis Presley on an old vinyl record cover, a guitar around his neck, both hands on a silver microphone, lip curled in his familiar pose. James removed it carefully and held it for a moment, then reached back in and picked up more records – Tina Turner, The Supremes, Stevie Wonder, The Beatles, ABBA – it was Mrs Samuel's precious record collection. Sally reached for the note and read it out loud to Paul.

"Oh gosh, I think he's right, James. These will mean a lot to you," she said.

James noticed there was something else at the bottom of the box. He reached in and pulled it out. It was a blue notebook – tatty, with curled corners. On the front cover the word 'Dances' was written diagonally across the page in what looked like a teenager's handwriting. There were some doodled musical notes and some instruments too – a guitar and drumsticks. James flicked through the book slowly. On each page there was a date from the 1960s and a venue – Parr Hall, the Cavern, the Memorial Hall, Mersey View, Royalty Theatre and many more. Underneath the venue there was scrawled writing, some of it almost indecipherable, but each one started the same:

To Julia.

To Julia, Enjoy the show, Gerry Marsden
To Julia, Thanks for the help! Dusty Springfield
To Julia, Best Wishes! From Little Richard
To Julia, Hope you liked the show, Roy Orbison
To Julia, See you at the next one, Billy Fury
To Julia, Thank you! Aretha Franklin
To Julia, What a great gig! Mick Jagger

Nearer the back there was a fading black and white photo taped to the page. It was a man in a suit with black dicky bow, and he held a trumpet in one hand. The photo was signed:

'To Julia, what a wonderful world, Louis Armstrong'.

James shook his head slowly. It was Mrs Samuel's autograph book. As he turned to the last page, he gulped.

To Julia, The Beatles number one fan. Love from John, Paul, George and Ringo.

Before he could say anything, his phone buzzed. It was Tom. He'd sent him a photograph of a business compliment slip:

To Tom,

I've had a word with a few people at one of the hospitals I work for. You should be getting a date for your operation within the next few days. I've booked you in for some intensive physio with one of the best in the business, she said you should be ok if you work hard at getting fit again. Good luck getting yourself strong so you can resume your football career.

John

"It's Tom, he's…" But James's phone pinged again. It was Malika. She also sent him a photo:

To Malika,

I've arranged some sessions with a local singing teacher, she'll come to your house to make it easier for you and your parents. I've also had a little chat with Laura and booked you in a couple of gigs at the care home. I know it's not Wembley, but you've got to start somewhere. You have to do some Beatles and Elvis though, for Mum.

John

"Oh, I've got a message from John," said Sally, interrupting James's astonishment as he stared at his phone. "Let's have a look…

Dear Sally, when I messaged you a while ago and said that your son wasn't normal, I was right. He's far from normal. He's like the golden rose he gave to Mum, he stands out from the rest of the bunch. I really respect the care he has shown towards my mum, something I needed to try harder with. He has taught me a lesson in kindness.

I had a word with the care home to see if Mum could have her record collection there – I know she misses it. They said there wasn't the room and I know James will look after it so well. However, I

have donated her old record player to the residents'
lounge so that James can take a record with him
to the care home whenever he visits and they can
listen together. Looking forward to speaking to Paul
tomorrow.

Best wishes,

John."

"Well, that's a turn up for the books," chuckled Paul. He stood up and joined James who was looking through the albums. "He's... he's right though, James. We're so proud of you. I'm proud you are my son. I understand. I understand everything and I'm sorry," Paul said, his voice catching.

James smiled. He hugged Paul and suddenly felt overwhelmed – there was a lot to take in. Picking up the autograph book and tucking the Elvis album under his arm, James plugged his earphones in and scrolled his playlist for Bob Marley.

"I think... I think I'm going for a walk."

Activities

Book Detectives

Chapter 1

📖 What has happened to James's friendship with Tom and Malika? Why has this happened?

📖 In what ways has James found the start of his time at high school difficult?

Chapter 2

📖 How did John Samuel make James feel? Can you find evidence of this?

Chapter 3

📖 What did James do to help himself cope with the school day?

📖 Why does James appear not to like Mr Ramos very much?

📖 Find verbs which help to show what mood Paul is in when he's making the cup of tea.

📖 Why do you think Paul tightly closed his eyes after his exchange with James?

Chapter 4
📖 Find evidence which tells us what type of character Mr Ramos is.

📖 Do you think James has changed his initial opinion of Mr Ramos?

Chapter 5
📖 Find all the evidence to show James sensed something was about to happen to him.

📖 Why do you think James's response was to march off after the pear was thrown at him?

Chapter 6
📖 Why do you think James chose to return to his old school?

📖 Find reasons why James felt embarrassed in front of Mrs Shah.

📖 Find evidence that Mrs Barton was feeling impatient.

Chapter 7
📖 Why did James become angry with Paul? Why did James respond in this way?

Chapter 8
📖 What type of characters are Uncle Jeremy and Auntie Denise? Can you find evidence?

Chapter 9
📖 What were the main things James noticed when he first saw Mrs Samuel again?

Chapter 10

📖 Why do you think Mrs Samuel always had a comment to make about the photos of Harry's grave?

📖 What do you think Cliff means when he says, "Today is a good day"?

Chapter 11

📖 Find reasons in this chapter why James respects Malika so much.

📖 How did James feel when Malika asked him what was wrong with him?

Chapter 12

📖 Why did James find the scene in the residents' lounge so lovely?

📖 What do you think James wanted to thank Cliff for when he said "for...you know"?

Chapter 13

📖 Why did everyone stare at Uncle Jeremy at the dinner table?

📖 Why do you think the tension had lifted on the way home?

Chapter 14

📖 Why do you think Josh charged in on Tom with a bad challenge?

📖 Why do you think the boys let the door swing to a close on Tom?

📖 Why did Josh snigger at the end of the chapter?

Chapter 15
📖 How were Mr Ramos's and Tom's reactions different when James finished the race, and why?

Chapter 16
📖 Find words that show James and Paul were angry in their reactions.

📖 What might Paul realise when he remembered he was the quiet one?

📖 How did Paul's chat with Reverend Varga help him?

Chapter 17
📖 How do you think James felt reading Sally's text responses to John Samuel?

📖 What does James mean when he says he is "losing her a bit" when he discusses Mrs Samuel with Cliff?

Chapter 18
📖 What is a Parish Council? Does your local area have a Parish Council? You could find out what they do.

Chapter 19
📖 With an adult's permission, you could do an internet search of 'old gravestone types' like James did.

📖 See if you can find out what some of the symbols on old gravestones mean.

📖 Why did James conclude that gravestones are 'beautiful works of art'?

Chapter 20

📖 How did Mr Adamson give away his interest in James's envelope?

Chapter 21

📖 Why do you think James suddenly told Mr Ramos his actual name?

📖 Why has Tom's injury 'levelled out the balance of power' between him and James?

📖 What provoked James's outburst to John that Tom was a good footballer and Malika was a good singer?

Chapter 22

📖 Why didn't James like free dress days?

📖 Why didn't James like sports gear?

Chapter 23

📖 How do you think James felt when Mr Adamson told him he was scared? Why?

Chapter 24

📖 Who was Louis Armstrong? You could research his musical achievements.

📖 Why did Cliff say the rose had helped Mrs Samuel remember?

📖 Why do you think Mrs Samuel liked "What a Wonderful World" so much? You could listen to the song and sing along with the words.

Chapter 25

- What do you think 'without fear there cannot be courage' means?
- How was Mr Fossington-Smythe feeling about James's speech as Paul delivered it? How do you know?
- Can you think of a word to describe the way Mr Fossington-Smythe addressed James?

Chapter 26

- Why do you think the girls were watching Malika and James talk?
- Why did James feel 'melancholy' about the afternoon?

Chapter 27

- What do you think it means, 'Malika knew the surprise would send James in a spin'?
- When John and James stopped under the lychgate, what do you think they were saying?

Chapter 28

- What do you think Malika means, "you've shown just about everyone how to be confident"?
- How have James's opinions of John Samuel changed through the story?

Chapter 29

- Why didn't James want to be mentioned in assembly?
- Can you find out anything about the people who have signed Mrs Samuel's autograph book?

What do you think Paul means by 'he understands'?

When James says he is 'going for a walk', where do you think he is going and why?

Acknowledgements

I am indebted to Val Campion (Mum) for the tireless and invaluable proofreading and editing advice. I really appreciate your support.

Once again, thank you to Catherine King for the time and effort you put into your wonderful illustrations.

I am grateful to family, friends and everyone who gave me encouragement and advice throughout this project.

About the Author

Keith Campion is a primary school teacher from Cheshire. He is a proud father to his young sons. *Flower Power!* is the sequel to *The Flower Boy*, and is Keith's third children's book. His first book, *The Last Post*, is used in schools as part of their English and history topics, and has been adapted into an educational touring theatre company production.

About the Illustrator

Catherine King is a retired teaching assistant who now has time to spend on illustrations and lots of other artistic hobbies. In addition to drawing and painting, Catherine likes to make sculptures from felt and handmade dolls' houses. She loves to create things for family and friends, as well as the challenge of taking on commissions and teaching skills to others.

Also by the Author

In a gentle way, you can shake the world.

James frequently needs to escape, to walk the streets of his local village and lose himself in his thoughts. James isn't finding his final year at primary school easy, and he wishes he had a brain that allowed him to chat and laugh like his classmates. Having spent his life avoiding trouble, it now seems to follow him wherever he goes.

When he stumbles into Mrs Samuel in the churchyard one autumn day, nothing is the same again. For Mrs Samuel, the present is a blur but the past shines clearly in her mind. Her tales about the village's history bring the past to life and ignite something deep within James. Without realising it, Mrs Samuel helps turn James's world from black and white to colour and inspires him to become... The Flower Boy.

But as Mrs Samuel loses her smile, will James find his?

KEITH CAMPION

the
LAST
POST

A poignant short story of
love, hope and legacy
during the First World War

*"We were all just desperate men who wanted to
be home for Christmas with the ones we loved; our
hearts torn between the duty to our country and
the warmth and shelter of our families."*

The wartime correspondence between a son and his father during the Great War. As 1914 draws to a close, William's letters are full of hope. Well they said the war would be over by Christmas, didn't they?

Helpful questions for
discussion and First World War
research ideas included.